Hot Chocolate and Holiday Mishaps

SAMANTHA PICARO

Books by the same author

Limitless Roads Café
Recipe for Confidence

CHAPTER I

Holiday tradition: decorate the tree

It is better to stand out than in with a Christmas tree. Our unique tree proves just that.

Mom and I sit on the empty plastic bins that had contained the ornaments and look at our handiwork on our fake tree (saving the Earth is important) in our onesies (mine is a penguin and hers is a polar bear). Our foyer, containing an elegant fake crystal chandelier, doors set with glass, and an antique armchair upon which a teddy bear with a Santa hat sits, is somewhere between classy and cozy, the coziness coming from the bear as well as a lily pad painting I made in second grade that isn't exactly museum-worthy and a grayish-white carpet as soft as feathers.

Mom and I admire the tree. Mom wanted to do a candy theme, so we went to town with candy-themed ornaments like gingerbread men, giant lollipops, and puff balls. The look is completed with pink Christmas lights and pastel gnomes holding fake candy canes under the tree.

"It's so bright it almost hurts my eyes," I say.

Mom takes a picture. "You know you love our tradition of making the tree as…unique as possible." I laugh with her because it's true. Last year we did a forest theme with things like small bird houses and woodland creature ornaments, and the year before that we used only recycled ornaments.

Mom turns the phone back to us so Bianca can see our laughter. In the background is her apartment with nary a decoration in sight except for a throw pillow with a Christmas tree pattern. She pulls the same wavy brown hair we all have into a bun as she says, "I agree. You outdid yourselves. It sucks I wasn't there. I would've chosen a movie-themed tree covered in popcorn, fake cameras, and other things."

"We'll still do other things when you come," Mom reassures her. Bianca nods but grinds her teeth. I curl my toes in my fuzzy socks and squeeze the handles of a pair of scissors when I think of the changes this year and Bianca's undeniable loneliness in that empty apartment. Her skin is pale with dark circles under her eyes.

Squeezing things anchors me as though the object prevents a tornado of negative feelings from sweeping me away, and I would squeeze pens in my failed job interviews for part-time jobs. Seeing my sister, older than me by six years, so miserable is definitely stressful.

"So, I actually have to tell you something." Bianca fidgets and hums. "My boss, Jane, is coming. She wants me to work while I'm there."

I scowl. "For real? Does she not get what taking time off means?" Jane Keller is a manager for celebrities and Bianca is her assistant. She's not the monster in movies who forces Bianca to pick up her dry cleaning or calls her words that can't be repeated on television. However, Bianca tells me she often is told how she screwed up and told us that Jane said that she can't keep "coddling" Bianca, that being autistic doesn't give her a pass. Bianca had to beg Mom not to call Jane or track her down.

"Didn't you take time off?" Mom frowns.

"I actually want to do this. Maybe I can finally prove myself. I've told you I've messed up lots of things." She has told us how she's mixed up schedules for two different celebrities, forgotten to bring materials to a meeting, and has left out or misheard details while taking notes for a phone call. It's mistakes I've made, too, at other jobs. One boss scoffed when I tried to explain how I do better with visual learning than auditory instructions. "Any other boss would've fired me, so say what you will about Jane, but she keeps giving me chances."

"Anyone else would make mistakes, too. This is your first job as an assistant to a manager."

"But Ellie and I mess up more than most." She looks to me, not insulting me but stating the truth. We struggle with verbal directions, get told our handwriting is chicken scratch, we're either too friendly or too distant with coworkers or people we're helping, and often need people to double check something even when we're sure because we're so afraid of screwing up. Then we get in trouble if we don't have someone double check or approve something.

I list all these things to Mom, who sighs. "I know. But you said you're getting better, Bianca?"

"Yeah, but I can still always go the extra mile. I need to do this."

"Well, why is she coming here? I didn't think big managers came to small towns like ours," I say. "There's nothing here except lots of potholes."

Bianca taps her fingers until I remind her tapping is one of the noises that drives me up the roof. "I'm watching her client, Robin Darcy, to keep her out of trouble."

Robin Darcy is someone famous but the type of famous where one may need a moment to recall her name. The eighteen-year-old has been in mostly TV movies. She's only had a leading role in three shows: a fantasy one when she was elementary school age, a teen drama that lasted two seasons, and a police procedural that had one season.

"Like a babysitter? Is that all she sees you as?"

Mom nudges me with a shush. "Are you sure that's a good idea? I don't want Jane taking advantage of you. Also, that Robin girl seems like trouble."

"That's why we're working on improving her public image. I'm guessing you saw that video?"

Who hasn't? Robin went to an outdoor market in New York, where she lives. Someone took a video of Robin shoving a man in a Santa costume and screaming, "This is why I hate the holidays! I guess I'm just another trinket to everybody."

The Santa fell into a stall, which knocked another stall, and so on in a domino effect. Chaos reigned as people snatched free items that fell and scattered from the stalls, police escorted Robin away, and pigeons feasted on scattered food like popcorn.

"She's been accused of being cold, if not a troublemaker," Bianca says. "I'm not breaking confidence because most of this has appeared in news. Coworkers say she's critical of scripts and what other cast members do, ex-boyfriends and -girlfriends say she's emotionally distant and always the one doing the breaking up; she even broke up with someone right before Christmas. An anonymous source said Robin is forced to go to functions, where she often disappears. People say she rarely smiles and she has no friends. People online are calling her a Grinch."

"Rarely smiles and has no friends? You know that describes us, right?" I point out. I'm annoyed on Robin's behalf. "You and I get accused of being emotionless because we don't express ourselves the way neurotypicals do. Neither of us has many friends either."

"I know that. I'm just saying what other people are saying."

Mom raises a brow. "And how are you supposed to watch this girl? What if she shoves *you*?"

"I'll be fine. We'll go over all that when we arrive. Jane and I are coming to your house if that's okay."

Mom and I exchange a look. Mom says, "Fine, but if she is a bully, I'm calling her out and you can just find another job."

"Mom, in this economy, it's far from easy even for a neurotypical person," Bianca groans, rocking side to side. "I have to go. I'll see you both soon. Love you."

She hangs up. Mom stands up and rubs her forehead. "I knew this job would be too much. She should've started by working for a manager with less prestige."

I pick at my shirt. "Nobody else would struggle this much."

"You two need to stop saying things like that. Yes, it's harder for your two but as I always remind you, non-autistic people struggle, too."

"Yeah, but it's not the same, and you're just invalidating what we say."

"I'm sorry. I just hope this isn't a disaster. Hopefully, Robin gets her crap together. Enough of that. Let's go back to being jolly. We can go to the café."

I agree, though it's tiring pretending to be fine. I have masked less in the past few years but it's hard to stop such instinctual things such as saying I'm fine. Also, the things that have me down aren't things Mom doesn't already know, like being friend-less and wanting friends despite liking being alone. My life has as many contradictions as politicians who preach coming together only to speak against certain groups.

The handle of the pen digs into my palm, making me hiss. I think happy thoughts like seeing Bianca (even if she has to work), spending time with Mom (and only with her), and ideas for my blog (which only has ten followers including Mom).

"This calls for hot chocolate. It makes everything better," Mom says, already grabbing her coat off the coat hook.

No arguments from me. Hot chocolate is our comfort beverage. It makes a hard situation bearable and is part of our bond.

*

The café is one of the highlights in Madison Grove, and not just because caffeine is inseparable from American culture and my and Mom's ability to function. We're lucky to live in a town where almost everything is within walking distance not only to save the environment but because I'm still a nervous driver especially in snow and ice; I freaked out when I tapped a garbage can in our driveway, although, to be fair, I never got over tapping cones while practicing driving with Mom and failing the driver's test the first time.

It's only two days after Thanksgiving and there are already garlands with bulbs wrapped around the lampposts like pretty snakes topped with wreaths, the potted shrubs are adorned with lights, and lights border almost every shop window. We pass a Santa asking for donations until we see a cop haul him away, stating the guy has no permit and "It's too early for scams, man."

Doris's Café is a medium-sized place between a bagel shop and clothes store with a wreath on the door, lights bordering the window, and even more holiday cheer inside. Small bows decorate the dividers between booths, a small white tree holds the wishes of low-income children in a corner, and strings of lights adorn the wooden order counter and to-go counter. The display case makes my mouth water from the vanilla cupcakes and brownies to the quesitos and tembleques. The seasonal specials like sugar cookies with frosting containing symbols of Hannukah, Christmas, or Kwanzaa are out.

Mom and I order our usual: hot chocolate. We add the seasonal topping option of chocolate drizzle, whipped cream and a snowman-shaped marshmallow. We treat ourselves to flan too. We take the last available table.

The owner, Doris Rivera, comes by the table as we wait for our orders. Her black curls are in a high ponytail with a red scrunchie and bright red nails nearly scrape my back as she hugs me then Mom.

I gesture to the surroundings. "Isn't it early for holiday-themed clothes? November hasn't ended yet."

Other people might find me rude when I say stuff like this, though I don't know why, but Doris laughs. "I love your honesty as usual. It's never too early. You put up your Christmas tree, didn't you? You don't think that was too early?" When my eyes widen and I look away, Doris says, "Ha!"

Mom and Doris chat while I take off my gloves and whip out my phone to look at my blog. *Ellie's Film and TV Reviews* has the least original title but I like to think the rating systems for tropes and diversity for movies, including TV movies, help it stand out, thus ten Followers instead of zero.

I go to a teen comedy movie released on a streaming network that Robin starred in. I haven't stopped thinking about her since our conversation with Bianca. I want to refresh my memory of this post and others relating to Robin. If she is a troublemaker or an ice queen, I want to know she's at least worthy of my sister's help, albeit through assisting Jane.

If she is mean to Robin, I'll call her out anyway because I've

never mastered "the game" especially regarding other girls but

I stopped trying to be neurotypical after many failed attempts

at socialization and work.

I look at the tropes I listed for this movie: fake dating,

insecure girl gains confidence, nerd and jock fall in love, small

town, you get the picture. The trope rating was three out of

five stars but the diversity rating was two out of five stars for

having two people of color characters, no disability

representation, and one gay character who fit the gay best

friend stereotype with no goals of his own.

The fun facts, another staple of my blog, include the

fact that Robin was not the first choice for the role because

they didn't know if "Robin could pull off being sunny and

energetic" due to her typecasting as snarky and rebellious and

her real-life persona. However, her manager convinced the

team to let Robin try out and they were pleasantly surprised.

Typecasting indicates Robin shares the personality of her characters but people could be wrong. I'm hoping everyone is wrong because I don't want someone bullying or just being snippy with Bianca. People get frustrated with us, and I get that our so-called quirks and mistakes are frustrating, and we should be held accountable. But is it okay for people to always make us feel worthless?

Hot chocolate squeezes out of my cup that I was squeezing. "Crap!" I shout, wishing I'd chosen something else to stim with. "Sorry!"

Emilio, Doris's son, helps me clean up the mess on the table and floor.

"It's okay. We get spills, like, twice a week," Doris says. "Emilio, why don't you tell them the good news?"

Emilio doesn't meet our eyes, which I know are the same hazel as his mother's as he stands. He also shares her high cheekbones and golden brown skin tone but he doesn't share her confident stance. "I'm playing my guitar at open mic.

Mom said I would, or else she'd make me attend as many holiday parties as possible. Ellie, I'm sure you understand."

I groan. "I can't imagine. For what it's worth, I'd like to hear you play."

"You don't come to open mics."

I shrug. "Maybe I will. I try new things all the time."

Mom nods. "That's true. I still remember the mess you made from painting and decorating that birdhouse in our yard. Sometimes I wonder if I should cut you off from movies and shows."

She's referring to the fact that I try new things that I see in movies or shows, whether it's an action movie (but non-life-threatening stuff like taking a self-defense course) or a wholesome family film (taking a pottery class). I put the activity I try or plan to try on each review on my blog. You'd think telling people I attended a glassblowing demonstration would increase my likes and followers but, alas, no.

"Maybe you should try it," Doris tells Emilio. "Get out of your comfort zone."

"I'm doing that already by performing," Emilio says with an eye roll. "You don't have to keep telling us autistic people to get out more."

She lightly taps the side of his head. "Don't roll your eyes at me. I mean try even more things. You might meet new people."

"Way to shame me for my lack of friends in front of people." But he smiles.

My stomach knots because I can relate all too well. I feel the need to defend him. "All the things I try haven't made me new friends. One, I still stink at making them, and two, having fun should be enough."

I get up to go to the bathroom as Mom asks Doris how her mom and cousins are doing in Puerto Rico. Alice Tanaka, one of the employees, passes me with a tray of hot chocolates. "Hi, Ellie! How are you?" She's more festive than Doris with a fake diamond-studded green headband crowning her wavy black hair, green eye shadow making her light brown eyes pop, and tan cheeks and toned legs from constant hikes and jogging even in the cold (which I know from the few times I have had the guts to make small talk) glittering gold from bronzer.

We're both seventeen-year-old high school juniors and love this café, but we couldn't be more different, fashion aside. Alice is in many clubs including the volunteer club I dropped out of, and she has worked here for at least a year, so she's not terrible at jobs like I am.

"Good. You?"

"Same old. Super busy but the tips are great, so no complaints. So, I read your blog. It's so good! I'm going to tell my friends about it."

I feel warmer than I did drinking the hot chocolate. "You did?"

"Of course! I looked it up after you mentioned it. I watched that movie you recommended a few weeks ago, *Do Revenge,* and loved it!"

"I'm glad. So, what do you think of the things like the diversity ratings, the activities I try, and all that stuff?" My hand is squeezing the purple stress ball in my pocket. Squeezing stuff is one of my stims, and Bianca gave me this stress ball last year for Christmas. I'm surprised I haven't broken it by now. Talking to people my age stresses me out.

"Amazing! I'm surprised you don't have more followers. I'll share it on my socials. Oh! I should deliver these hot cocoas before they get cold. Talk to you later!" She rushes to a table.

I smile on my way to the bathroom, a rare occurrence given that smiles are often to show others how one feels. I feel as bright as the golden bow at the top of the mirror, hoping I shine just as bright by gaining more online attention.

*

A made-for-TV movie is the best way to end a cold day.

We're snuggled up in snowman blankets with matching penguin socks in our living room watching the typical scenario of a corporate lady learning to appreciate the things that matter in a small town with help from a handsome farmer. No, wait, in this movie he's a plumber. But it's the same gist of a woman abandoning a lucrative career for a town she only spends a few weeks in and for a guy she just met. Bianca, Mom and I love these movies but they're a guilty pleasure for a reason.

I love these movies for the hope and heartwarming themes as well as the awesomely decorated sets. If Mom could hire someone from these sets to decorate our house, she would. Bianca quickly got over the embarrassment of a slipup she made scheduling a meeting for Jane when she learned that she would accompany Jane to a holiday movie set. One reason I look forward to her visit is she is sneaking us a holiday decoration she swiped from the set. Normally, breaking a rule, let alone a law, would have us hyperventilating but we can make exceptions for holiday movies.

Mom doesn't mind that I type notes for a review on my phone as we watch. I'll praise the heartfelt atmosphere as usual with this type of film while reminding readers that one doesn't have to give up everything to find happiness and belonging, and that romance isn't the only way to change your life. Readers can get annoyed that I bring up for the thousandth time how much attention the love interest gets for helping someone change but bonds with new friends or reconnected families get nowhere near the same amount of attention. A comment on a previous post called me a bitter aromantic and said aromanticism is fake, which took me days to get over despite knowing not to listen to trolls.

This movie is one of the most diverse I have seen: the two main characters and most of the cast are Black, there are two characters in a same-sex relationship, and there is even a teen wheelchair user, whom a quick online search confirmed is played by a disabled actress. People also get tired when I keep writing about the progress movies still have to make with disability and neurodivergent rep.

"I think I'll try ice skating," I tell Mom.

Mom groans. "Don't break your back just for your blog."

"It's not just for the blog. It's to prove to myself I'm adventurous." My hands clench into fists at the thought of ending up in a hospital or making an ass out of myself.

Mom notices and snorts. "You look so confident."

I roll my eyes. "I have to try. It's something we can try with Bianca if she's not too busy."

She purses her lips. "We can't know how busy she'll be watching after a star. But fingers crossed."

I squeeze the blanket as I contemplate how much different this holiday season will be despite Bianca returning.

CHAPTER 2

Holiday tradition: Last-minute gift shopping

Lunch is my favorite part of the school day.

I get to eat and do whatever I want while sitting with someone who doesn't make me talk. Hilary Griffin and I sit at our usual corner table in the cafeteria, which I swear is a little more in shadows than anywhere else as though to emphasize our invisibility. It's pathetic considering the cafeteria is literally and metaphorically bright with its eye-burning lights, motivational posters, and a glass wall exposing the forest for our viewing pleasure, though all to see are thin trees almost stripped bare of brown and auburn leaves, fallen branches, a thin layer snow with brown dots of dirt like bald spots, and litter.

Hilary's red lacquer nails tap on her phone with her face hidden behind ash blonde hair while I listen to a videogame soundtrack as I make a list of ways to market my blog. Online wisdom advises me to use hashtags, share to my Stories, interact with other accounts, use trends, the usual. Which I have already been doing. Disappointment weighs down my chest like a chunky squirrel testing his weight on a tree outside the glass walls.

"What are you up to?" Hilary asks, blue eyes not looking up from her phone.

I pull off my headphones, wincing when someone releases a booming whoop from a nearby table. Why do people think loudness gets their point across more? "Ideas to increase engagement on my blog. I've been doing what they recommended like commenting on other posts, following relevant accounts, posting at the statistically proven best times for engagement…"

Hilary holds a ring-clad spray-tanned hand up. "You're babbling again. We talked about this. And you talk about stuff you're passionate about, which is fine but you still sound so…monotone."

I tend to go on tangents even if it's not a special interest. Hilary alerted me to it in a previous conversation when I gave what she called "lectures" on the origin of holiday traditions. She also said people might get put off by my monotone. I was so humiliated I bit the insides of my cheeks until they hurt as Hilary explained that things like this is why people may be "turned off by me." Bianca wanted to yell at Hilary when I told her about this but I reminded her it's true. Also, Hilary and I never hang out outside of lunch so I doubt Bianca will meet her. We sit with each other to avoid the stigma of sitting alone at lunch.

"Have you started gift shopping?" Hilary asks. "I need advice for a gift to get a new friend."

She has a friend? If she's getting this person a gift, will she get me something?

"What do they like?" I ask.

"Video games, so what can I get? I can't afford a console or anything like that."

"A gift card makes gamers happy. I play games, and I love picking whatever game I want with a gift card. Or you can get a shirt or hat with their favorite game character on it."

She shrugs. "I can do that. Thanks."

I ask before I lose my nerve. "Did you, uh, want to exchange gifts?"

Hilary freezes with her mouth parted. Then she shrugs. "If you feel like it."

I've mastered the art of telling when someone is just being polite. I swallow the lump in my throat. "No, it's fine. I don't' have a big budget. I can bring cookies to lunch."

"Awesome!" She stands, flipping her blonde hair over her shoulder. "That friend asked me to sit with her, so is it okay if I go?"

She's not inviting me to sit with them? Seriously? Screw her. "Go ahead. I'm going to the library."

She leaves without another word. She forgets the uneaten candy bar she bought, and I keep it for myself out of spite. It's also one of my favorites.

We're not friends but it hurts when people don't invite me to sit with them. I would've done it for her. I blink back tears and eat the candy bar as I remind myself that at least I didn't get her a present without talking about it. In the past, I've gotten gifts for people I thought were friends only to get nothing in return because they didn't think we were friends.

I focus on Bianca's arrival tonight. My pulse races as I contemplate meeting Jane and Robin.

*

The house is cleaner that it has been in…well, ever. We have vacuumed the entire first floor, cleared the living room of non-guest-worthy objects like our slippers and blankets. She has placed a tray of homemade pignoli cookies (of which we already swiped two each) on the coffee table. She slaps my hand when I try to take another.

"You should be flattered I enjoy your baking that much," I argue.

She chuckles. "Your grandma would've been pleased, and Lord knows it was almost impossible to please her." She bites her lip and looks away. We rarely talk about my grandparents, who don't like that Bianca and I are autistic or that Mom doesn't do whatever they tell her to. "The one good thing that came from my parents was the passing of traditional Italian recipes."

We sprayed air freshener from the TV stand to the patio doors on the opposite wall that reveal a small square yard with a swing set I still sometimes use and leaves and twigs covering the dry grass like brown, gray and dark red sprinkles.

I hum and sway to a pop holiday song to soothe my nerves. If I stim, it may as well incorporate holiday cheer. The nerves explode like fireworks when the doorbell rings, causing me to chug water from a snowman mug in the kitchen. I place it down without a coaster despite Mom's insistence on protecting the granite kitchen island and race to the foyer.

Bianca's cheeks are red, but it's not entirely due to the cold and I doubt it's from cheer. Black circles are carved underneath her eyes, she's thinner, and her eyes shift to the two people with her like she expects to be eaten. She's wearing her puffiest white coat; she wears large and/or puffy outfits to feel secure. She's twisting her fingers as I sometimes do, but she does it more; her hands and wrists are red.

Jane Keller intimidates me with her pinstriped jumpsuit that is somehow sharp like knives at every edge including the shoulders, heels that could poke holes in the floor, a brown chignon with blonde highlights, flawless tan skin, and dark red lipstick. She exudes confidence as she shakes my and Mom's hands.

With them is Robin Darcy. She's as tall, slim, and fashionable as she was in that disastrous video except now her blonde hair is covered with a dark wig and her azure blue eyes are hidden until she takes her sunglasses off. She's on her phone without acknowledging any of us.

Jane swipes the phone from her. "Don't be rude. They're helping with your second chance."

"I shouldn't need a second chance," she says. "I also shouldn't have to disguise myself. That wig is itchy." She scratches her head.

"We've had this conversation a hundred times. Now, be polite and say hello."

Robin doesn't smile as she says, "You already know who I am."

"I'm Claudia and this is Ellie," Mom says. She takes her hand back when she realizes Robin won't shake it.

"Hi," I say in a squeaky voice.

Jane's eyes fall upon our tree and she does a double take, making Mom chuckle. Robin's lips twitch as though holding back a smile.

"That is a very…interesting tree," Jane says.

"Better to stand out than in. Otherwise, I wouldn't sell so many things on my online shop. Now let's sit down."

We go into the living room. Robin plops onto the couch and munches on a cookie. "Damn, this is good."

"At least pretend to be professional," Jane scolds.

"Why bother? The world already thinks the worst of me. And it's a compliment. This doesn't taste like the stuff you get at stores."

"I made it. It's a family recipe," Mom says proudly.

"You're Italian?"

"My father was an immigrant and my mom was the daughter of immigrants. But let's get right to business." Mom will find any excuse not to linger on the topic of my grandparents. I don't like thinking about them either, especially when I recall how Grandma told me other kids would be nicer to me if I acted more normal. I was five, by the way, and Grandma didn't seem to care that I'd just been called an animal for growling at the others to express my frustrations and the kids teased me with animal noises.

The rest of us sit more gracefully and I'm the only other one to take a cookie. Jane matches Mom's don't-mess-with-me-or-my-daughters stare with a raised brow.

"What a lovely home, Mrs. Conti," Jane says. "I wish I had time to decorate, but there are never breaks for a manager. People think celebrity managers just book movie roles but I do everything under the sun." She ticks off the tasks on her fingers bedecked with crimson-colored nails sharp enough to hurt someone. "Hiring people like publicists, organizing media exposure, financial guidance, and suggesting classes to take even if you're already a decent actor. Last but not least, I help clean up messes." She glares at Robin, who rolls her eyes.

Mom keeps glancing at Bianca, who literally stands behind Jane every step of the way, still wringing her hands. "It's Ms. Conti. I went back to my maiden name after my husband left, and my girls wanted to take on my name, so I let them." Mom shrugs; hardly anything fazes her, let alone talking about uncomfortable parts of the past.

Bianca and I glance at each other. I don't often think about our dad except when I see other people with their dads or watching movies with the dad I wish I had. He left when I was three because he couldn't handle having two autistic children. I don't remember him enough to miss him; it's more like I miss what could have been. I munch on a cookie to focus on the delicious almond taste rather than my psyche.

"So, what exactly is Bianca supposed to do?" I ask.

Jane raises a thin brow. "Right to the point. I respect that. I had a different idea because Bianca will help me with everything else. And don't worry; she'll have time with all of you. I want her to have time with family."

This is a good sign. A she-devil wouldn't be so considerate, right? I look at Bianca but she doesn't deflate with relief like me. With a nod from Jane, she pulls two pieces of paper from her purse.

"You have to sign these before we discuss anything. It's no big deal," she says quickly.

"Relax, Bianca. You're talking too fast, and you look like you're being chased by a bear," Jane tells her, placing a hand on her shoulder.

Mom takes the pieces of paper. "NDA's? For what?"

"Just read them over. They're just related to Robin," Bianca explains. "You just can't discuss Robin with people without permission, and you can't discuss anything we talk about."

"Doesn't sound that complicated," I say.

Mom insists on reading through them before allowing us both to sign. "So, what's going on?" she asks.

Jane folds her hands in her lap. "You've heard about the incident and Robin's overall reputation as an ice queen. For the season, people have added 'Grinch' to the mix."

"And that's just the PG-rated stuff," Robin mutters.

Jane ignores her. "Bianca has talked about her town and I figured a place like this would be perfect for a PR makeover. Robin will do different activities around the town to restore her image, and it will also bring attention to the town. Everyone wins. But rather than Bianca making sure Robin stays in line, I was thinking someone closer to Robin's age could do that."

"I'm not a freaking prisoner," Robin says, slapping her hands on her knees.

"Do you want to improve your image or not?" Jane says coolly. I push myself into the ouch with the hungry look Jane gives me. "I was thinking you."

I'm frozen. "What?" I look at Bianca, who scoots closer to me to squeeze my shoulder.

"I told Jane it might be too much," she explains.

Jane waves her hand. "Your sister doesn't have to do much other than stay with Robin at each event and keep her company between them. She can make sure Robin doesn't do anything ill-advised."

"I've, um, explained to you how we get tired easily from being with people and not getting alone time," Bianca says, not meeting Jane's eyes and somewhat mumbling.

"Then you two can take turns. I understand your…unique needs, and I've accommodated you, haven't I?" I can't tell if Jane is annoyed or not.

"Yes, and I appreciate how patient you've been with me, even when I, um, put too many typos into a letter to a producer."

"Is this heartwarming moment over? If so, can we just call this whole thing off so I can go home?" Robin demands.

"You're not that lucky," Jane tells her. She turns to me. "What do you say? Just stay with her, make sure she doesn't get into trouble or that trouble doesn't find her, and keep her company if Bianca and I can't. As you can tell, Robin doesn't care for friendship, so you don't have to worry about needless things like conversation. Besides, you can ask us for a favor, within reason, whether it's an internship gig or a visit to a film set."

"It's your choice," Bianca assures me.

Mom leans in to whisper to me. "You should do it." She rolls her eyes at my own widened pair. "You need to get out more, and I've never been strict about what you do because I know you're responsible." That's true. Mom often complains that I'm *too* responsible, whereas she's the type of mother who swears more than we do, let me watch PG-13 movies as early as nine years old, and groans when I do the exact speed limit.

My toes are curled so much I'm afraid I'll break them, and my body is boiling hot from the pressure to accept. Even if Robin is fine with no small talk, will she bully me? Will she make me fetch her coffee? Will I have to protect Robin from a stalker?

But Bianca is counting on me. She helped Mom raise me since our crummy dad took off. She would do this for me. I can get over my intimidation by a celebrity.

Also, Jane was right that I might gain something from this, but I don't care about her suggestions. This arrangement might benefit my blog.

"I'll do it," I say, mouth as dry as autumn leaves.

Bianca's smile is genuine for the first time this visit. "Thank you so much!"

But Robin's frown gets deeper. "No offense, but how can someone like her babysit me? She seems timid and like she has zero experience with celebrities."

I glare at her, nerves replaced with embarrassment but also anger. "Don't talk like I'm not here. I don't have experience with stars, but the job shouldn't be that hard. All I have to do is tell Bianca or Jane if you've done something 'ill-advised' as Jane put it. I don't think you want to risk more bad press anyway."

She rolls her eyes. "Whatever."

Bianca speaks with more confidence. "I'm helping Jane prepare the events around town that I proposed as well as interviews." She takes a moment to blush and revel in Jane's approving smile. "We don't think security will be an issue in a small town and given that Robin is not as big a name as people think."

"Hey!" Robin looks stung.

"Honey, you know it's true," Jane says. "So, it's settled! Let's go over the events."

Bianca brings the schedule up on her tablet. Robin will stay at the hotel when I'm not with her, and cannot go anywhere alone because even a not-so-big-name celebrity needs to be careful. I'm told not to post pictures or videos of or with Robin without approval. I'm to keep Bianca posted of our whereabouts at all times even though we both have the Find Me app. I'm not to go anywhere with Robin without permission from Bianca or Jane. Robin is to wear a disguise outside events. I write everything down in my Notes app.

"Will this leave Robin any time with her family?" Mom asks.

Robin stiffens. "I don't really do the holidays anyway. We're not a holiday family, so it's no prob." She doesn't meet anyone's eyes.

Mom purses her lips but says nothing. They don't celebrate the holidays? That sounds so sad.

After a few hours, they leave. I grab Robin before she leaves as Bianca, Mom, and Jane talk. "I hate to ask but may I ask a small favor?"

"Asking for favors already? I thought you'd give me the courtesy of at least waiting." Robin narrows her eyes at me.

I wince but blurt out, "Will you tell people about my blog? It's called *Ellie's Film and TV Reviews*. Not the most original name but it's got unique things like diversity rating system, an activity I try from each thing I read or watch, and stuff like that. Maybe help from someone like you can boost its exposure? That's all I want in exchange for everything."

Robin's eyes furrow in confusion. "Seriously? Not a selfie, money, or a role in a movie? This is a first."

"I don't care about that stuff. Will you consider it?"

Her silence gives me hope until she crushes it like a Christmas ornament under a boot. "I'm done doing people favors. Sorry but no. See you when you're babysitting me." She storms out, leaving me feeling like a fool for the second time today.

Bianca sees how stricken I am because she asks Jane if she can stay, which Jane allows. "How about a movie night with hot chocolate and popcorn?"

"I had hot chocolate today, so I should watch my sugar intake but yes to the popcorn," I say.

Mom tells us we can watch a movie while she finishes paperwork; her online craft shop, job as a masseuse, and an inheritance from Grandpa after he died lets us live comfortably. She's such a good masseuse, talented crafter, and lovable person that she has been featured in the town paper, especially for her specialty in oncology massage, hosting craft sessions for children and adults with disabilities, and donating a portion of her online shop earnings every year to a charity of her choice; this year, it is going to the animal shelter. Before we became estranged, I had "the audacity," as my grandma put it, to ask her why she and grandpa couldn't see how awesome Mom is. To this day, I feel it was a valid question.

Minutes later, Bianca and I sit on the couch with popcorn to watch *The Holiday*, one of our favorites.

"So, your boss doesn't seem like the heinous woman I thought she'd be," I remark.

Bianca laughs. "No, she's not heinous. Sometimes she's harsh but I deserve it." She holds up a hand. "I'm allowed to be criticized for making a mistake. Of which I've made many, like mixing up meeting dates. I really am doing better at my job. Jane praised me for coming up with the idea of the public image makeover."

"I can't believe I agreed to watch Robin. I don't know what I'm doing. She'll walk all over me! Or she'll sneak off and I'll get blamed if something happens to her." I breathe heavily while squeezing a pillow.

Bianca reminds me to breathe and rubs my back. "I'm here for you. We've got this. We Conti women can get through anything."

"But I screw things up all the time. I quit before I could get fired from two jobs. I dropped out of every club I tried or was 'asked' to leave."

"Those things weren't right for you. I got fired from my first assistant job, remember? Now I found one that's right for me. Robin may seem tough, but Jane and I haven't had to twist her arm too much to do anything. You'll be fine. This is the season of miracles, after all."

"Then maybe I'll get the miracle of no more homework before December even starts," I joke.

"And I'll find a new boyfriend or girlfriend before the New Year."

She hugs me as we watch the movie. Even the direst circumstances are better with my big sister and the butteriest popcorn.

CHAPTER 3

Holiday tradition: cookie decorating

Cookie decorating is a little different this year.

Every year, Mom, Bianca and I decorate cookies with the PTO and other students for residents at the local nursing home. This year has seen a spike in signups due to Robin's presence. Bianca insisted that it would show how fun and generous she is, to which Robin scoffed before Bianca dragged her into the small gingerbread brown brick building that is the rec center. The gymnasium floor is as shiny as the fake glittery ornaments on garlands strung up on the walls above flyers and hand-drawn pictures by kids. Objects like the air hockey table have been pushed to the walls to make room for the tables covered by trays of sugar cookies and decorating materials.

"So good to see you back, Ellie," Mrs. Gable, head of the PTO and a volunteer at the nursing home, says with a smile as bright as her cherry-red sweater and green eyes that always twinkle. She squeals and hugs Robin, who winces. "And it's awesome to meet you! We're so honored to have you here. You took time out of your busy schedule to help us make the holidays brighter for the nursing home residents."

Robin forces a smile for local reporter George Thomas and a camerawoman. George smooths his buzz cut and smiles to show off his pearly whites and high cheekbones. Mom has (grossly) gushed about his attractiveness, specifically his tallness, auburn hair, and freckles all over his fair face.

Robin gives the speech that Jane and Bianca rehearsed with her. "Of course. A colleague told me about Madison Grove, and I wanted to see the charming town for myself." Bianca rolls her eyes. "I wanted to try something different for Christmas. I'm no expert at cookie decorating but I'm here to have fun and give back." Her appearance is supposed to make her appear approachable and humble too: hair piled into a bun, natural-looking makeup with lip gloss, and a white sweater.

George asks, "Will your parents spend Christmas here with you? Rumor has it you don't speak to them."

Robin doesn't bother smiling anymore, making Bianca twist a loose curl. "That's far from the truth. We just don't see each other as often as we'd like because of my work. They're supposed to spend the holidays with me and my aunt, so fingers crossed the weather doesn't cancel their flight." She crosses her fingers, but her eye twitches. "Let's get to decorating these cookies!"

Robin and I go to a table; each table is big enough for two volunteers. Some of the girls from school try to get her attention. But Robin turns her attention to me, surprising all of us.

"Talk about anything. Literally anything. Just talk so I can pretend I'm engaged in conversation already," she whispers. "I'm not in the mood to talk to fans."

I shrug while trying not to take offense. "So, I know some cool Christmas facts."

The girls turn away and talk to each other after a minute or so. Robin says, "All of that is true? Even how stockings became a tradition because a saint dropped gold coins through a chimney into girls' stockings to pay their dowries?"

"Yup. You weren't bored? I can get carried away."

"I like random facts." She looks at the cookies. "Have you done this before? You're good at this, and that PTO lady recognized you."

"I've attended classes at the center before. I like to try new things." I don't mention how most of it is inspired by the blog as I still feel the sting of Robin refusing to promote it. "What's different this time is you, obviously, plus I'm usually alone."

"Alone?" Robin doesn't say it like she pities me, which other people tend to do.

I hide my flushed cheeks by turning to get a green piping tube. "I'm a loner." I'll let her assume it's by choice.

"So am I. At least we have that in common. I still can't believe I'm doing this. Could you help me come up with an excuse to get out of this?" She glares at me when I smile. "I'm serious."

"I don't think we should. This is supposed to boost your image."

"And maybe I can earn sympathy by faking an illness."

"No."

"God, you're no fun. Maybe that's why Jane stuck me with you."

I glare at her. "Or maybe you're just used to getting your way. Well, today is a new day, so suck it up and finish decorating. It looks like you could use the practice."

All she's done is make each cookie an entire color with very uneven stripes. Not even the dots she put between the lines are the same sizes. I've gone simple with snowwomen with black dots for eyes, eyelashes and lips, carrot noses, and blue hats.

She focuses on her cookies with a huff. "Yeah, well, who cares if they're ugly? Everyone should be happy I'm even here. I get enough criticism, so why don't you keep your thoughts to yourself?"

"Fine, as long as you do the same."

"Fine."

A few minutes later, a volunteer named Candace, Alice's older sister, is impressed by our work. Robin smiles as she gestures to cookies made to look like green or blue presents with lines and a red bow in the middle.

"This is amazing! Ellie is a great teacher," Candace says. She tucks her chin-length black hair behind her ear. "So, um, is Bianca back in town? I was hoping to see her." Eyes that are same light brown as Alice's sparkle while her cheeks turn as pink as her sweater.

"She's…doing work stuff." I catch myself before I break the NDA. "But if you have her number, you can text her, right?"

"Oh, right, right. I just didn't know if she was busy. I'm pretty busy myself with the gift shop because of the season." Candace is a manager at the shop her mom opened before Alice was even born. "Anyway, I'll check out the other cookies." She rushes off with a swish of her long black ponytail.

Robin laughs. "Oh, she's got it bad."

"What do you mean?"

"She likes Bianca."

"Oh." I wish I could tell these things. "Then why doesn't she just ask her out?"

"Haven't you ever been nervous asking someone out?"

I squeeze an empty piping tube. "I'm aromantic. You probably don't know what it means."

"No, I know. And sorry for assuming. You'd think I wouldn't assume people's orientations as a bisexual woman but I guess I'm still human." She shifts on her feet. "I, um, read your blog. You review a lot of rom-coms. Is that odd as someone who is aromantic?"

"You read my blog?" Maybe there's hope of her helping me after all. "It's a little weird. I'm reminded of how I don't fit society's expectation of finding happily ever after with someone. But I can enjoy those things without romance for myself. I also enjoy side plots, the things happening on the side. For example, in lots of romance books or movies, the heroine isn't just falling in love; they are looking for a job or adjusting to a new town."

Robin nods. "I would often annoy directors and castmates by pointing out flaws in a script, like how the love interest in one of my movies was actually a toxic guy hiding behind the nice guy mask. I had to spend a few days at a spa after filming finished because I was disgusted with myself for acting in it."

My eyes widen. "That's terrible. Is that why people say you're difficult to get along with?"

Her jaw tightens. "People say lots of crap. Are you another hypocrite who loves thinking they know everything about me?"

I shrivel under her gaze. The edge of the piping tube cuts into my hand so I'm forced to drop it. All I can say is, "I'm not sure what to believe. I just know celebrities, especially women, are judged harshly."

She turns away. "You have no idea."

"Judged harshly? Your actions speak for themselves." The speaker is Jamie Smith, a fellow senior in lots of extracurricular activities. She crosses her pale arms as she stares down Robin. "Maybe people wouldn't judge you if you hadn't pushed Santa."

Robin crosses her arms. "Did you ever think to ask for my side of the story? Or are you another mindless follower of the entertainment business?"

"The same business that allows you to wear those expensive clothes and strut in here like you own the place?"

Jamie flips her wavy brown hair. "Decorating cookies doesn't make you one of us."

"I wouldn't want to be like you, anyway. Go shove a cookie in your mouth."

"I guess the moniker 'Frost Queen' isn't too off point." She shares a cackle with her friend.

Green icing shoots Jamie in the chest. She gasps then growls as Robin smirks. Jamie squeezes red icing onto Robin's hair, and the girls get into an icing fight. Robin ducks and the icing meant for her gets onto a guy's cheek. He throws sprinkles and hits all of us.

A food fight ensues. Sprinkles, icing, and small candies fly through the air. I hide under the table as I'm unwilling to engage. The loudness of the shouts and shrieks are made bearable with the candy I stuff myself with. I swear I can hear Robin cackle.

You'd think the adult volunteers would stop this. They are even more merciless than the teens. Mom says PTO members can be competitive, so I shouldn't be surprised to see them facing off against each other.

A whistle blows. I peek from under the table. Mrs. Gable lowers the whistle, her normally ruddy cheeks now as red as a fire engine. "What is wrong with all of you? You're adults, or young adults! You've wasted food on something juvenile and made a mess. I will not have the janitor clean up your mess. Clean up now and make sure at least some of these cookies are presentable enough to send to the nursing home. Shame on all of you!"

Bianca escorts us out but it's too late. The photographer caught everything and takes pictures of our exit. Bianca forces us to sit in her car, grimacing and cussing as the icing on our clothes and hair gets onto her car seats and floor. She didn't escape unscathed either as proven by a red piece of icing that drips onto the console.

She's wringing her hands and shaking as she yells at us. "What the hell were you thinking? Jane's going to be pissed! Oh, god, oh god." She takes deep breaths that don't calm her. "I have to call her."

She goes outside where she paces while she calls Jane. Acid bubbles in my stomach as I pray Bianca doesn't lose her job.

"It'll be fine. It's not the most scandalous thing I've done. Remember the story where I was caught smoking underage at a children's TV awards show? I was just trying to alleviate stress." Robin speaks softly like she's speaking to a scared doe.

For once I don't care about making someone mad or uncomfortable. I snap at her. "You couldn't just ignore Jamie? Are anger management issues another thing you have to convince people you don't have? My sister could lose her job!"

Her mouth hangs open. She turns away to stare into her lap. "I'm sorry," she mumbles.

Gone is the cold, rude girl I met last night, replaced by someone who looks like she wants to curl into herself and disappear. I know the feeling all too well from disappointing people, so I say, "But I think what you did was awesome. Jamie is a huge jerk."

Robin grins. "I regret nothing. You hid under the table like a coward."

"I was being smart. I took advantage of the situation to eat some of the candy."

We laugh. Robin wipes a tear from her eye because she was laughing so hard. "I haven't laughed like that in a long time. It feels good." She clears her throat. "I can bring attention to your blog. If you still want me to."

"Really?" This had better be real or I might faint from the stress of the day.

"It's the least I could do for putting Bianca in hot water, probably you too. It's not the biggest favor someone ever asked of me, so why not? But can I ask why you wasted your reward for babysitting me on that? You could've gotten an internship like Jane offered."

"I don't think I'd be good at movie stuff. I want to be a critic someday. The blog is just practice. It would look good on a college or internship application if the blog went viral. It's also just precious to me. It's the one thing I'm good at. I stink at other things."

Robin gives me a long look before taking out her phone. "I can share some of your social media posts right now and tag you. Even the hypocrites who call me an ice queen can't resist what I share."

I blink back tears. "Thank you so much."

She wags a finger at me. "Don't think this means we're friends or anything. I'm just doing what's right. You're still an unwanted presence."

Insults usually sting but I'm too happy about my blog to care. "And you're still a grouchy celebrity."

Bianca taps on the window so I roll it down. "I have to help Jane do damage control. Take Robin home or somewhere if she's in disguise. Just lay low," she begs, still shaking.

I place a hand on hers. "I've got this. Robin, do you mind walking? Everything is walking distance."

We get out of the car and begin the walk home. Robin puts a brown wig and sunglasses on. Her shoulders are hunched. "I'm good at messing things up. That's the one thing the tabloids get right about me." Her voice cracks. "Maybe I should put a stop to this pointless project because nobody expects anything good from me. I could cause another scandal right now."

I inhale sharply as my brain provides an unwanted montage of possibilities: getting into a fight, taking off, ranting on social media, you name it. My chest hurts and my fingers squeeze the front of my jacket as I try to figure out a way to talk her out of it.

"Why don't we change clothes at my house and we can get hot chocolate?" I suggest. "A good hot chocolate always cheers me up. It's the ultimate comfort snack."

Her forehead creases in thought. "I don't feel like having people get up in my face. I doubt anything can cheer me up. Hot chocolate doesn't have that much power."

"Don't underestimate its power. Then wear the disguise and a really big coat. You can borrow my clothes. You're way thinner than me so my clothes will be loose on you." I step in front of her so she's forced to stop walking. "Just please don't do anything reckless. I don't think any of this is pointless. Plenty of famous people come back from scandals." I don't care that I'm begging. I can't disappoint Bianca or fail at yet another thing.

She ponders it then shrugs. "Oh, what the hell. You're so terrified of disappointing Jane that I feel bad for you. I won't cause any trouble. I promise. Just stop looking like you're about to have a heart attack."

*

Nobody recognizes us at the café except Alice, who says, "Don't worry. I won't tell anyone. I never understood everyone's obsession with famous people. No offense."

"None taken. Actually, that makes me happy," Robin says. She moans after taking a sip of her hot chocolate. "This is amazing!"

"I told you so." I sip my hot chocolate that is smothered by whipped cream, blue sprinkles, and marshmallows shaped like polar bears. Robin takes a photo and shows me my whipped cream mustache and goatee.

"You could add it to your social media Stories just for giggles, though I see you've been doing just fine getting more followers," Alice says.

"You still pay attention to my stuff?"

She chuckles. "I'm not the type of person who says something to be polite and doesn't do what they said they would do. But it does bite me in the ass with group projects. You should think about coming back."

I bite the inside of my cheek. "I never really fit in there. I'm also not good at clubs and stuff. Fingers crossed my blog will become impressive enough for colleges to beg me to attend. If not, I'll just have to explain in applications I'm not the talented, good-with-people type." I look at the polar bears rather than the people who must think I'm a loser.

I rush to the bathroom before I cry in front of anyone. After four minutes, I come out after my eyes are dry and less red. Alice is chatting with her friend Nicole Williams, who is just as well-rounded but has leadership positions and volunteers at the library, which I frequent. I doubt she'd recognize me because I never talk and I rush out as soon as I check out books. Like Alice, she's big on holiday accessories as proven by the Christmas-themed scrunchies adorning her two black puffy buns.

I have to go past them back to my table. They smile at me. I can never tell if smiles are genuine or just polite, so I can't help the nervousness. "Hi," I croak. God, I'm pathetic. I'd be less intimidated by piranhas than my female peers. Then again, past experience has taught me teen girls can be way more dangerous.

"Hey. You're Allie, right?" Alice's friend says, taking a sip of her iced coffee. The dark brown eyes that observe me are adorned with bright red eyeshadow and gold glitter brightens her light brown cheeks.

"Ellie," I correct her. "You work at the library."

"Volunteer. It'd be nice to get paid but I still love it because books are my life." She chuckles. "I see you there often. You're so quiet when I check out your books, like you can't wait to read them or go."

"Um, yeah." Is she the type to think I'm a loser for frequenting the library? Is she offended that I don't try to make small talk at checkout?

Alice says, "Ellie has a blog about movies. She shares stuff from lots of book blogs on her socials. Maybe you can talk her ear off about reading and let me off the hook. You know I'm a super casual reader. Like, two books a year for pleasure."

"Oh, really? I'll have to check it out. Send me the link. I have to get running. Story time waits for no one." She turns to me. "Bye, Ellie."

"Bye."

Alice crosses her arms once Nicole is gone. "I wish you weren't so shy. I can tell you have a lot to say. Nicole says you never say more than two words when you check out at the library."

"I'm not a talker and sometimes people say I'm interrupting their work when I try to chat. It happened at places I used to work and at school. It's not worth it."

"Some people are jerks but I guarantee that Nicole and I wouldn't feel bothered. I just have to go now before that kid spills her iced tea. I can predict these things; this job has made my psychic. By the way, I have an online art store you could check out. I draw, sketch, paint, you name it."

"Sure! Send me the link, since you follow me."

The kid spills her iced tea like Alice predicted. That's impressive. What's also impressive is how I consider her advice to give socializing another chance. Yet I can't stop worrying that it's too late for Nicole and Alice to see me as anything besides a quiet loner.

I hesitate to return to the table as I see Robin writing in something. She writes something with a fuzzy purple pen into a narrow notebook the same height and width as her phone. The notebook slams shut as soon as Robin sees me approach. She stuffs the notebook and pen into her ridiculously huge bag with the force Mom uses to stuff turkey.

"What was that?" I ask after sitting down.

"Just doodles. Do you have to know everything?" she snaps. "You might have to watch me but you don't get to peek at my stuff like a jailer."

"God, relax! It was just a question."

I doubt they were just doodles, with how embarrassed she was to be caught. But she's right that it isn't my business, plus why should I care?

"Just take me back to the inn," she demands.

"Okay, Your Highness," I mutter.

CHAPTER 4

Holiday tradition: snowballs

The inn is a combination of creepy and jolly.

Decorations from Halloween are incorporated into the holiday decorations but not in a cute *Nightmare Before Christmas* kind of way. Furry bats with blood red eyes wear elf hats, mistletoe and holly are placed in the eternally open mouths of screaming skeletons, and fake jack-o-lanterns wear Santa hats on the wood steps. The only solely holiday-themed items are the garlands twined around the rails and columns of the porch.

The owner sighs when I walk into the foyer with Bianca, where the decorations are horror-free. "I'm sorry for the decorations. My daughter is bitter from my recent divorce from her mother, and I promised she could be in charge of decorating," he says, rubbing his face. "Anyway, you can help yourselves to tea and biscuits while you wait."

We sit on a floral couch in front of a window showing off one of the million little creeks in New Jersey where fallen twigs and acorns rest upon the ice. Bianca rocks back and forth like a rocking chair while I munch on a cookie from a tin.

"It'll be okay. Everyone thought the holiday food fight was hilarious," I tell her.

Bianca glares at me. "But do we need to make Robin look immature? My job is to make Robin look as good as possible!"

"Hey, it wasn't your fault."

Robin stomps down the stairs and blows past us out the door. We follow her, close the door, and look to see that nobody is around because Robin is yelling.

"I shouldn't apologize for sticking it to a judgmental, phony bitch!" Robin's face is as red as the evil eyes of the fake bats.

"Please, keep your voice down!" Bianca hisses, making a lower-your-voice gesture with her hands.

Jane's scowling face is on Robin's phone screen. "I'm just reminding you, Bianca, and Ellie to be on your best behavior. You're lucky people found the food fight more cute than scandalous."

"But I shouldn't have to apologize to that girl." Robin's nostrils flare.

Bianca's twisting her hands. "It's not that big a deal. It doesn't matter if you mean it. She said she won't go to the press and badmouth you if you say sorry. Please?"

"Don't beg," Jane tells her. "And next time, get a better grip on our client."

"It wasn't her fault," I say. "What was she supposed to do? Put a shock collar on Robin? Bianca is doing her best and Robin shouldn't have done what she did but, honestly, Jamie deserved it. Instead of harping on what happened, maybe just appreciate that things turned out as good as they did?"

"What you don't realize, Ellie, is that part of being a manager is being on top of this stuff, predicting what clients or others will do, something I know you both struggle with."

"I don't need your condescending tone."

Bianca shoves me out of the way. "We understand what you mean. Ignore her. The three of us are going to see Jamie."

"Get this sorted out. Then meet me to plan the next event and put out more fires."

Bianca whirls on me after ending the call. "I don't need you to defend me! You could've gotten me fired. Do you ever think before doing?"

I grab her hands before she twists her hands off. "Excuse me for standing up for you! She didn't have to be so mean about it!"

"Just go! You think you know everything? Take Robin to see Jamie. I'll help Jane with everything else. I can't look at you right now."

"You're not taking my car. I drove us here."

"I'll call an Uber!" She storms to the curb and presumably arranges for transportation on her phone.

Robin whistles. "Damn, that was intense."

"Shut up! You're apologizing and that's it."

"Like hell I am!" She takes off on a trail behind the inn that's flanked by waist-high boulders and trees that are almost stripped bare of autumn leaves. The joke's on Robin because the road just leads to town, so there is no escape.

We only make it a few steps before Robin throws her hands up. "This path leads to town, doesn't it?"

"Yup. Jamie lives on the border of town, so you'd be going her way anyway."

She growls and collapses on top of a boulder. "How small is this town? If I were in a city, I could disappear!"

"Yeah, 'cuz that would solve your problems."

"Shut up! You're supposed to keep an eye on me, not give unsolicited advice." She puts her face in her hands. "This crap is just too much. I hate saying sorry to people like Jamie, people who judge me without ever once wondering if my life is all it's cracked up to be. Did anyone ask me if I shoved that Santa because he kept saying inappropriate things and grabbed my arm?"

I inhale sharply. "He touched you? That is not okay!"

"Yeah, and I wish I'd shoved him harder or kneed him in the groin."

"I wish you had, too. Did you tell anyone?"

"I tried but nobody would listen. They only cared about the optics of shoving Santa." She groans. "I'll say sorry to Jamie. I'm used to humoring others, anyway."

"What happened to you is not okay. It's frustrating and sickening that this still happens to women." I rub my head then look at the snow. "Before we see Jamie, we could de-stress."

"How? With caroling?" she snorts.

"Even better." I create a snowball mixed with mud. Robin wrinkles her nose at it. I shrug. "In New Jersey, it's common to get plenty of mud mixed with snow. Make one and throw it as hard as you can."

"Seriously? This is juvenile."

"Try it. If you want, roll a rock into it. It's satisfying when something breaks."

I throw my snow-mud-ball at a tree. Snow and brittle brown leaves fall from the branches.

Robin shakes her head but rolls a stone in snow and mud and hurls it toward the creek. We heard the thud against ice and the angry screeches of birds.

We throw more snowballs and rock balls at boulders, branches, you name it. Robin laughs so much she can't stop, putting her hands on her knees as though she is out of breath. I join her laughter.

"That was silly but fun. I'm a little less pissed," Robin admits between giggles.

I wipe a tear from my eye. "This helped me when I lost my last friend, or who I thought was a friend until I tried giving her a gift and she said she didn't think we were that close."

"No way! That's really crappy," she says. "I remember when I was on my first show. Remember the one where I played a witch at a high school for supernatural and fantasy creatures and I had a pet unicorn? I thought my castmates and I were friends until I overheard a costar talk about me to another."

"I can't even imagine. I used to assume proximity equals intimacy, but rejection teaches me things really quickly. For what it's worth, I thought you were the best character and actress on the show. Don't give me that look. I don't say things I don't mean."

"I've had to become a pro at hiding my emotions. People don't like emotional actresses. Scratch that; nobody likes emotional women."

"I wish I were a pro at hiding what I feel, like when I had a meltdown last year because I got a really low grade in Math even though I technically passed. I tend to cry at school in front of people, which is super embarrassing. I went to my yard after school and threw rocks. I also did it when I finally realized I wasn't talented enough or interested enough in anything to stay in a club. I quit the last club I joined, which was a volunteer group, because nobody included me in conversations and thought I took volunteering too seriously, whatever the hell that means."

"Screw them. Screw that Santa. Screw everyone!" Robin raises a fist in the air.

"Screw everyone!" I throw a snow-rock. It sails toward a garden gnome in someone's backyard. I cringe at the *crack* I hear.

Robin says, "Run!" We run like hell but can't stop laughing. We stop and catch our breath once we're far enough away.

She frowns when she meets my eyes and clears her throat. "You're supposed to keep me out of trouble, not get me into it. That was fun for a minute but don't think this means I like you now. Let's head to that jerk's house and get the apology over with."

She walks ahead of me with a flip of her hair. She switches from hot to cold faster than a faucet. Her coldness after the fun we just had stings. However, I'm not supposed to be her friend. I need to stop caring if people like me or not.

*

Hours later, we're at the inn gorging on candy.

Robin insisted on sugar and movies after her apology to Jamie, who sniffed and literally turned her nose up like a snobby aristocrat but accepted the apology. She went on about how forgiving she was. On the way out of Jamie's house, I swiped one of many bags of candy from a dining room table that Jamie mentioned were in preparation for a school function. Robin "accidentally" knocked over one of the pots on the front doorstep and we dashed as soon as we heard it break. Hopefully, Jamie will think it was a squirrel.

We devour the candy on Robin's cream-colored bed in her tiny but cozy room which even has a fireplace, albeit electric but still toasty.

Robin has control of the TV. "I can't have alone time except at bedtime because you, Bianca, or Jane is always with me or calling me, so the least you can do is let me have unlimited control of the remote."

"You don't think it's narcissistic to watch your own TV show?"

We are watching reruns of Robin's teen drama, where she played an heiress who starts a new life in a beach town and moves in with her aunt after her parents go to prison for embezzling. We're on the third episode ever in which her character runs into a former classmate who teases her about her circumstances until one of her new friends stands up for her.

"Not really. I like this show and not just because I'm on it. I thought the plot was meaningful and most of my costars were nice, though I tend not to get close to people." She rubs her arm as though confiding something so personal gave her chills. "Be real with me. What do you think of this show?" Robin asks.

"Well, I didn't watch it when it first came out because it was award-worthy. It's a comfort show and something you don't have to pay too much attention to. Plus, your character, Rachel's troubles remind me things could be worse."

"Gee, thanks. At least you're not as harsh as the critics." She flops onto her back with a groan. "I'm so freaking bored."

"That's the third time you've said you're bored. You have a better idea for entertainment?"

"I do, actually. There's a club in a town nearby. We can take a cab."

The idea of breaking the rules, let alone going to a club, makes me feel as hot and itchy as if someone threw a fuzzy blanket on me. "I'm supposed to keep you out of trouble."

"Oh, please. I've managed at clubs before."

"Jane and Bianca would kill us." I clench my phone so hard. "I wouldn't be good at watching you if I allowed it. I'm also not great at parties. I hate them, actually."

"Come on. It's just one hour. I haven't asked you for much." She crosses her arms. "Everyone wants me to find holiday cheer. I'll be less miserable stuff if I get to have a little fun."

Can she not see my agitation in my refusal to meet her gaze or the way I press myself against the headboard in the hopes I'll fall through it into another dimension? "No clubs."

She shrugs. "Fine. Then I guess you don't want me to make a video saying how awesome your blog is."

I'd feel as bright and energetic as a firework if not for the catch, which brings me down like rain. "And you'd make me go to a club for that? Can't I do something smaller?"

"I'll sweeten the deal. I'll take a selfie with you and tag your account."

"I don't really do selfies or personal stuff." The thought of people seeing me the person makes my stomach as acidic as tomato sauce.

"People like feeling connections with creators. Trust me, I know, even if people like Jane won't let me reveal the ugly truths of fame. There's nothing in your About Me section except your age, your state, how much you love TV and movies, and that you want to be a professional critic. Give them more of you."

"I don't know." The acid gets worse until I have to swallow bile.

"You're using this blog to get noticed as a critic, right? I'm assuming you want to add this to a resume or something? No offense but having less than a thousand followers won't impress future employers. Come on. Going to a club won't kill you."

"It might," I choke out.

She turns my face to meet her eyes. "Ellie, it might also do you good to get out more. Live a little. What do you say?" She holds out her perfectly manicured hand.

Writing reviews is the only thing I'm good at, the only thing that I'm confident about. I would be a fool to turn down this offer. I shouldn't be such a baby about people potentially judging me. Robin is judged all the time and she gets by.

I shake her hand and rush to the bathroom with the diarrhea that always comes from intense agitation.

CHAPTER 5

Holiday tradition: wear winter-themed jewelry

The only jewelry I can tolerate are loose bracelets and necklaces. Otherwise, I feel choked or uncomfortable. I wear a candy cane pendant to go with an elf costume that is more sexy than cute and refuse the earrings Robin offers to let me borrow.

This outfit is one of the ones Robin has "just in case" there is a party. She's donned a brown crop top with fuzzy gum drops and frosted edges with a matching skirt ending above her knees to show off her slim legs. A brown and red gingham headband that rests on her silver wig completes her gingerbread look. Brown contact lenses complete her disguise.

She gently unwraps my fist from around a poor defenseless stuffed bear with a snowflake bow. "Is this how you, um, stim? Is that the word?" I nod, to which she says, "We'll be fine. Nobody will suspect a thing. Just one hour."

"It's not just that. This is my first sleepover since middle school. I've never had an easy time sleeping anywhere but my bed. I can't even fall asleep on a plane despite being exhausted and miserable. I have to take two melatonin gummies to sleep over." My face is as hot as the electric fireplace.

"We'll figure something out. Hey, it's nothing to be embarrassed about, so lose that look. I don't sleep easy either." She looks away then clears her throat. "Let's head out before we go feeling sorry for ourselves."

I drive so slowly that Robin groans until I speed up a little just to shut her up. Driving takes my attention away from my volcanic stomach acid and hot, itchy skin. Luckily, the roads are almost empty in a place like Madison Grove and even in the town over until I reach the street with the club.

Miraculously, there is one parking spot left in the parking lot that I take forever to back into.

"Thank god! I thought we'd never get here. And you don't have to be so nervous about tapping cars." Robin hops out, stumbling in her heels.

"This remind me of that TV movie you were in where the two friends handle the one friend's grief over losing her dad to a drunk driver by sneaking into a club. You're not getting déjà vu?"

"Well, we're not friends and nobody died, so not really but I guess there are some similarities."

I wince, even though we really aren't friends. I guess I'm not the only person who can be really blunt, although the difference is that I think Robin intends her words to sting whereas I generally (key word: *generally*) do not. Just because we're not friends doesn't mean she has to sound like she's stuck with me. Then I remind myself that technically she is.

The line to get inside isn't long, so we don't have to freeze outside for too long before we're stamped with "Under

18" on our wrists and hurry inside. The building is a former warehouse with tons of space, a second floor, and holiday decorations from the balls dangling from the rafters to the Christmas-themed lights on the walls.

The music is so loud it vibrates against my body as I collapse into a booth. I rub my arms to get rid of the goosebumps that came from having to squeeze past so many strangers and ignore many lustful gazes. A waitress dressed as a sexy candy cane takes our orders, a lemonade for me and water for Robin, then leaves us.

Robin stands. "Come on. I'll get us real drinks."

"How?" I point to the stamp on my wrist.

She blows a raspberry. "Like that's hindered people before. I'm excellent at persuasion. Come dance and flirt with people. OH, wait. You're aromantic, right? Are you asexual?"

"Yeah, and I'm sex-repulsed. Go have fun. I can wait here. I might vomit if I move too much. You're lucky I agreed to this." I push myself farther into the booth until I'm against the wall.

"I'm not leaving you alone in a bar." She crosses her arms. Her eyes soften when she sees me looking at our surroundings like a scared doe. "Hey, are you that scared?"

I stare at the crude drawings on the table. "I have anxiety. It's common with autism. I'm literally anxious about being here. I'm doing this for my blog and I'm terrified Bianca and Jane will find out, or a guy trying to kidnap me or some other true-crime scenario." There is no pause between my words.

She grimaces. "Damn. You should've told me. Just because I hate you keeping an eye on me doesn't mean I want anything bad to happen or for you to feel unsafe."

"If you just sit here all night with me, then we would've come for nothing. You're also not the nicest company." I raise a brow at her scowl. "You know it's true. Maybe you can socialize where I can see you?"

She purses her lips then nods. "Okay. I'll be in sight. Get me if you have to go to the bathroom." She gets up to flirt with a girl where I can see her.

I stare at my phone, not only wanting to get out of here but people are staring at the loser sitting alone at a bar. I don't mind being alone, but it agitates me when people stare at me for being alone, if that makes sense. But this is better than dancing with zero skills; last time I tried dancing at a high school party, I was told I was too stiff and I accidentally elbowed someone. Never again. I also cringe at the thought of little to no personal space.

My heart rate returns to normal as I squeeze my stress ball and research my next animated movie to review, a tossup between a Netflix original and a movie released in theaters, when someone takes my headphones off. A guy in a Santa suit that's open to reveal his abs grins at me across the table.

"Hey," he says. "What's a cutie like you doing alone?"

"Not much." Yup, I suck at these things. Then again, I don't want to interact with anyone. Even if I were allosexual and alloromantic, I'm only here to fulfill my end of the deal.

I tell him as much, to which he laughs. "You're funny. As if those aren't made-up orientations to make people feel special."

It's not worth trying to educate him; that rarely succeeds. I also have too much of a headache from the music and stress to care if I'm being rude. "Look, I was forced to come here, so please go. You seem nice but you're wasting your time on me."

He takes my hand. "Don't be so rude, or you'll end up on the naughty list. Then again, it's the naughty people who have the most fun." He winks.

"Creep!" I yank my hand away and snatch my headphones. He calls after me as I scurry off. Where is Robin? She said she'd remain in sight but I can't see here anywhere. I breathe heavily as I squeeze through the crowd. The rushing of my blood drowns out the music and laughter as it usually does when I'm super anxious.

I go into the alley because it's getting too hot in there. I exhale in relief when the freezing but refreshing air hits my skin. I lean against the wall despite the risk of germs.

But the sounds of panicked breaths tell me I'm not alone. I spot Robin to my right, crouched and hunched over while trembling like an earthquake.

"Robin?" I lean over her.

"Go away!" she wheezes.

My annoyance with her for ditching me vanishes. "Damn! Should I call 9-1-1?" I ask, chest tightening.

"No! I get panic attacks. Talk. Say anything."

"Like what?"

"I don't care!" she snaps. "You're supposed to look after me, so calm me down by saying anything."

"Okay, okay." I rack my brain. I slide down the wall so we're on an equal level. My butt hovers an inch over the ground because I do not trust the cleanliness of this ground. My fears are founded when a rat goes by with a fry. Robin is so upset she doesn't notice but I need to help her calm down as much as possible.

"So, I crossed something off my bucket list tonight. I choose an activity from a movie or TV show I watched and try to do it. For example, I convinced my mom and sister to go to Salem with me after officially reviewing *Hocus Pocus*. Tonight, I can cross off going to a club. I remember adding that to my list after watching *Sleepover*. I hated it in there and a creep was bothering me but I can look at silver linings."

I barely pause between sentences because of my worry for Robin. Is my worry increasing her panic? But her breathing has slowed and her body isn't quaking anymore. I continue. "I tell people I don't mind doing things alone, and normally I don't, but it'd be nice to have more company. I want people other than Bianca and Mom to do things with. I know we're only spending time together because we have to but it's still cool. I can at least say it's never boring with you."

I ramble about holiday traditions around town Robin might like while rocking back and forth on my heels and squeezing my headphones. Robin looks at me with red-rimmed eyes, face as pale as the fake frosting on her outfit. She stands on shaky legs. I grab her before she falls.

"Thank you," she whispers. "I'm so sorry. I said I wouldn't leave you but I couldn't stay in there."

"Me neither. I felt like I was going to explode. May I ask what cause the panic attack?"

She rubs her arms. "Everything. I keep making the same mistake: thinking partying will distract me from my feelings. I wanted to escape my thoughts about the undeserved judgment from everyone, spending the holidays in a town I never even heard of until recently, and pretending to rediscover my holiday spirit when I never had any. I was reminded how alone I was when this creep was harassing me and asking me and the girl I was flirting with to have a threesome. Nobody stepped in to help us, so I splashed a drink in his face. He reminded me so much of my ex-boyfriend with his looks and his attitude."

She cries. "This would be the ex I broke up with during the holidays, the one who accused me of being heartless for doing so. I told my manager I wanted to share my side of the story, which is that golden boy Joey would always put me down, called me names, told me what I should wear, and said he didn't believe bisexuality is real. The last straw was when we got into yet another fight and he told me my movies sucked and accused me of using him to boost my status. He purposely broke an early Christmas gift I got him, a crystal angel to honor his dead mother, calling it cliché. It reminded me of what my parents did to stuff I gave them that they didn't like. I had a panic attack. When it was over, I realized he'd left."

I try not to cry. Yes, I'm the type of person who cries when other people cry. "That really sucks. He's a jerk. Does anyone else know?"

"My manager at the time told me it wouldn't look good if people knew I had panic attacks. He also said it was my word against Joey's, who is more famous and, honestly, more liked than me. My reputation as a cold diva had already been established by then. I'm also used to keeping things private."

She wipes her eyes. "Sorry. I totally unloaded on you."

"Don't be. Thanks for trusting me enough to tell me. No guy has the right to treat you like dirt. Are your parents why you don't like the holidays?"

She wipes her eyes. Her face regains its usual hardness. "I was vulnerable enough letting you see me like that. I'm not going to reveal my entire life story. I just want to get the hell out of here. And can you not look at me with pity?"

She stands on wobbly legs. She moves away from me when I reach out to help steady her.

My jaw clenches along with my fists. "I didn't have to help you, you know. I don't like people seeing me vulnerable either, but you don't have to be mean about it."

"Yeah, you did have to help me because you agreed to look after me. And does my attitude matter as long as your precious little blog gets attention?"

"So, I'm just supposed to take this?"

"Now you know what I deal with in the acting industry. Let's go." She stomps past me but yelps when she sees the rat from earlier munching on discarded chips. "God! How did I not notice?"

"You were having a panic attack and then yelling at me. We should go before I vomit."

*

This is more like it.

We're in fuzzy pajamas and savoring the heat from the electric fireplace. Robin laughs by how I'm on the very edge of the bed to enjoy it.

"Aren't you baking? I might turn it down." She tugs on the collar of her T-shirt.

I wiggle my bare toes. I like the feeling of heat on my cold feet. But I don't answer her because I'm still mad.

I hear her sigh before she crawls from her spot on the pillows to sit next to me. "You're not mad at me, are you? Look, I'm sorry. I just get embarrassed when people see me having a panic attack." She twists a strand of hair around her finger.

"You shouldn't be ashamed. You also shouldn't have to deal with disgusting men like the guy in the club, the Santa you pushed, or your ex-boyfriend. It sucks even more that so many people have told you not to talk about it. Just know that I'll always listen and try to be supportive."

"Thank you. I promise I won't ask you to do something like sneak into a club again. I'm not holding my breath about gaining holiday cheer, but maybe I'll get a movie script idea."

I look at her. "Movie script? Do you write movie scripts? Is that what you were writing in your notebook at the café?"

She tenses. "No, no," she says quickly. "I didn't mean movie script. I meant to say...Oh, screw it. Can't come up with a convincing lie. Could you forget I said anything?"

"Why do you hate talking about it?"

"Ellie, I've been through a lot tonight. I'd rather not discuss yet another thing that brings me stress. I mean, the act itself doesn't stress me but the idea of sharing it with people. Please?" Her eyes are wide.

I don't respond. She waves her hand in front of my face. "You still there?"

"Oh, yeah, yeah. Sorry. Sometimes I get lost in thought. I was thinking how I'm sensitive about my reviews and getting judged, so I get it. It's why I don't share personal stuff online. It hurts to have my work judged but hurts worse when I'm judged for being myself."

"If anyone can understand, it's me. I'm going to sleep. Let's pretend tonight was just a bad dream."

In the middle of the night, I wake up, as often happens in an unfamiliar place and after a stressful night. I see a notification on my phone screen. I'm sent to a short video Robin made raving about my blog and how it inspired her to try new things. "For example, I tried being open with someone about personal stuff. It was scary, but totally worth it." She shyly glances down, probably not used to being vulnerable.

I'm not used to anyone besides my family doing so much for me. She must have done this while I was asleep because she took the video in the hall and speaks softly.

I now have a few hundred more followers on my blog and social media platforms. I rarely express emotions except to follow neurotypical standards of letting other people know how I feel. But the joy can't be contained within me, shooting out of me through a wiggle my body does when I'm excited. I clap my hand over my mouth when I squeal so I don't wake up Robin.

CHAPTER 6

Holiday tradition: going to the mall

Robin looks like she's getting her teeth pulled in that interview chair.

I spend lunch with headphones plugged into my laptop to watch Robin's interview on the local news station. She jokes about the cookie food fight and spins it so that people think she's rediscovered fun. She announces she's going to volunteer to be Mrs. Claus at the mall this afternoon because Santa is busy. What she doesn't reveal is that the mall Santa had too much fun at a bachelor party the night before. Bianca had suggested it anyway and Jane hadn't fully considered it until now.

Patricia Jones, the anchor, laughs along and makes witty remarks. She's a legend in Madison Grove for becoming the first Black anchor and first to be open about having Bipolar I for our news channel. Her dark brown eyes twinkle as much as her snowflake pendant.

The interview goes well. They get along great, although Patricia can make anyone comfortable.

"As a woman, I get what it's like to be extra judged and being accused of either being too emotional or a Frost Queen as some people have called you, which is not right," Patricia says.

I could hug Patricia and I can tell Robin could, too. "You're the first person to say that, so thank you. I know I have it easier than women of color and a woman with a mental health condition, such as yourself, but I appreciate it."

Patricia's eyes widen. "I appreciate that, too. I try to be open to try to reduce stigma. I imagine you have to work extra hard now to change people's opinion of you. People who typically star in kid-friendly movies and shows tend to be expected to be perfect in real life."

"Oh, yeah. It's a never-ending job but it's important to let people know I don't hate the holidays and I'm not the frost queen they think I am. I value the holidays and what they symbolize." Too bad she means none of it; Bianca coached her. "After all, I've starred in countless holiday movies." That earns some laughs.

"It seems you've rediscovered the holiday spirit. Would a new friend happen to be another reason for that?"

Robin stiffens. "Why would you think that?"

"We know a local teen was with you at the holiday cookie decorating, and there have been reports of you walking around with a young female. No need to be coy. Is this a new friend, or even a girlfriend?"

I almost choke on my apple. My skin becomes hot and itchy as I will Robin to answer. Attention of any kind makes my skin crawl. I take out my stress ball.

"No, I'm taking a break from dating. This person is just part of my team."

Hopefully everyone buys that. I shut my laptop and take off my headphones when the interview ends, my body shaking. Hilary snorts. "What happened? You look pale."

"No, I'm just excited."

She frowns at my stress ball. "You still have that? You rely on it too much."

I could tell her that's a rude thing to say and she can't possibly understand what anxiety is like. But maybe I shouldn't assume the worst about Hilary. Nobody is perfect. I'm certainly not. Even if Robin isn't filled with the hope of the holiday season, I must be because I blurt out, "Do you want to hang out sometime? We could do something Friday or the weekend."

She leans back, eyes flitting left and right like I demanded she hand over her lunch money. She grimaces until she can manage a smile. "That'd be really cool but I'm super busy this weekend. So many projects before winter break, you know? Rain check?"

"Oh, sure."

Hilary flees before I can say anything else. I drink water to lessen the volcanic flush of my face. Part of me knew what the answer would be but I make the same mistakes over and over. I was right not to try making friends. I should focus on Robin duty and my blog.

*

The mall is one of my favorite spots to visit, especially in winter.

I'm not a big shopper; I frequent the mall to walk around and just look at stuff, plus the food. The holiday decorations never fail to wow me, from the red ribbon-adorned garlands to the giant ornaments dangling from the ceiling, although I sometimes wonder if any have ever destroyed Christmas cheer by falling.

Robin snorts at this thought. "If it would get me out of doing this, I'd be all for it. I thought it was horrible when I had to play a mall elf in one of my holiday movies but this takes the cake." She smooths out her Mrs. Claus skirt for the billionth time. We stand beside Santa's throne in front of the giant Christmas tree while a long line of kids waits to see Mrs. Claus. The red dress reaches the knees while striped leggings cover her legs and a Santa hat sits on her shiny hair.

"At least I look cute." She twists her fingers.

I grab her hands. "Don't twist your hands like my sister. I always worry she'll make them fall off. I'm nervous, too, and I don't even get to speak. Thanks again for making me volunteer." My sarcasm is as heavy as the invisible stone sitting in my stomach from being here surrounded by all these people with all these cameras. I jab at the knee-length green elf dress and pointed hat I was made to wear.

"I didn't want to be the only one in a ridiculous outfit. Also, maybe a petty part of me wanted you to suffer for being my unwanted bodyguard." She smirks.

"You jerk!" I give her my fiercest glare, which just broadens her smirk. "I hope you get the meanest kids."

"You'll have to deal with them, too, so my suffering is your suffering."

I groan, wishing my outfit had pockets for my stress ball. I settle for squeezing the fabric of my skirt instead (yeah, I know: hypocritical).

Someone signals it's time to start. Robin rubs her head before plopping herself on the throne. Bianca stands to the side and keeps glancing at us while talking to photographers and reporters. I give a wobbly smile to reassure her despite my body shaking more than a body in a massage chair.

Robin struggles to maintain her smile throughout a few incidents. One purposely farts on her, making everyone except Robin and I cackle. Another tells her that Mrs. Claus belongs in the kitchen, to which Robin tactfully replies that the Clauses have an equal relationship. A little girl's parents force her to spend two long minutes wiggling on Robin's lap deciding on what she wants rather than rush to the bathroom.

My role is to lead the kids to Robin and lift a child onto her lap if necessary. I definitely need to work out more because lifting kids is not as easy as one may think. Some kids don't let me lead them to Robin and they jump on her. The hardest part is getting kids to stay in line and keeping the line organized. Robin smirk at my hardships.

But it's worth it to see her hardships with unruly, farting kids. I don't know who's more frazzled or who smirks more at the other's misery.

Everything goes well until one child approaches with a golden retriever. The retriever sits by panting as the girl sits on Robin's lap to state her desired gifts. As Robin wishes the girl happy holidays, the dog stands, lifts its legs, and pees on the throne.

Robin ushers the girl off her lap with a whimper. She screeches when some of the pee gets onto her boot.

"Are you kidding me? You didn't take him out before coming here?" Robin's face is as red as her dress.

The girl starts crying as she holds the dog's leash and her mother wraps an arm around her. The mother glares at

Robin. "We did take him out. He just has a bad bladder. We didn't mean for this to happen."

"Why bring a dog at all? Dogs don't have gifts they want!"

Her voice echoes through the mall. She freezes upon seeing the judgmental eyes and harsh whispers. Some people are recording this.

"So it's true that she's grumpy!" a kid calls out.

"I'm so sorry," the little girl sniffles.

Bianca is pulling her hair as she thinks of a way to salvage this situation.

I shouldn't do anything. I could screw things up. But Bianca is too frozen to do anything. Robin looks at everyone like a deer surrounded by mountain lions.

"She's just stressed!"

All eyes are on me. I'm shaking so hard I'm surprised I don't collapse. I clench my hands. "Nobody likes stepping in dog pee. We've all been there, right?" I chuckle nervously. "You should understand why she was caught by surprise. But she's not mad at you." I turn to the little girl. "She was caught off guard. She's also doing a lot this month to help people have a cheerful holiday season. It's great to do good but also requires a lot of time and effort. Can you forgive Mrs. Claus?"

The girl considers my words before turning to Robin. "I'm sorry Bruce did that. Bruce is the only thing that cheers me up ever since my dad left, so I take him everywhere."

Robin's face softens. She bends so she is somewhat at the girl's level. "I'm sorry for yelling. I'm glad you have Bruce. It's not his fault that dogs can't use human bathrooms." The girl returns Robin's smile. "Why don't you finish telling me what you'd like for Christmas?"

The girl nods and tells her. I gesture for Robin to pet Bruce, which she does. "Good boy," she says.

The crowd goes "Aww". Hostility is replaced with admiration as Robin allows Bruce to lick her face. The girl's mother thanks Robin.

Bianca runs to us once it's finally over. "Thank you so much! Why didn't I think of that?"

"You really saved my butt. I shouldn't have frozen. Bruce really is a good boy." Robin fans herself with her hand. "It's freaking hot. Can I take this thing off already?"

"Of course. Good job to both of you." Bianca hugs me. "And I'm sorry about our fight at the inn. That wasn't cool. In the end, everything worked out. But I shouldn't have taken it out on you anyway."

"It's all good. Are things going okay for you?"

She shrugs. "I haven't messed up scheduling or anything, so that's a great sign. Jane texted me and says she loves how you saved Robin just now. She said both of us were doing a great job." Bianca's eyes water. "I rarely hear that. It's partially thanks to you."

One of the paparazzi approaches us. "Do you work for Robin? Are you an assistant?" he asks, holding a recorder to my face.

Bianca pushes it away from me. "She's just a volunteer."

Other people shout out questions.

"Are you part of Robin's public image makeover?"

"Are you the rumored friend?"

Bianca ushers me away with a protective arm around my shoulders. We make it to the changing rooms where Robin should be. I lean against the wall and hold my aching stomach.

"Breathe." Bianca tries to make me do a breathing exercise. She throws her hands up when I don't join. "Who am I kidding? It doesn't even help me."

"Did they get pictures of me? Will people bother me now? I'm not an attention kind of person." I slide down the wall, tucking my knees to my chest.

Robin exits a stall in jeans and a sweater. She sits next to me. "Tell me what you need."

I remember Robin's panic attack. "Oh, I'm not having a panic attack."

"It's okay if you are. If you aren't, I'll still help. I won't lie: people no doubt got photos of you. They'll wonder if you're the mysterious friend or girlfriend."

Bianca glares at her. "Seriously?"

"Lying won't help. I still get intimidated by cameras despite doing this for years. But they'll forget you quickly. It's me they want. They'll pounce on the next thing that grabs their attention. Just try to blend in. It's kind of my fault you brought attention to yourself but you don't need to save me. You're my sort-of-babysitter, not my guard." She laughs.

I look at her. "I don't regret it. That girl was a brat."

Bianca chuckles. "I never thought I'd deal with this situation when I took this job. But Jane says to be prepared for anything. Be glad this is the only day you have to be Mrs. Claus. Let's get you back to the inn."

We stand. Robin twirls a piece of hair. "Actually, can we just hang around? I don't want to leave just yet. I'm prepared before you say no." She takes a brown wig and sunglasses out of her ridiculously huge purse.

After a pause, Bianca sighs. "Okay. I'll let Jane know. But we're not staying too long." She looks at me. "Plus, I feel bad we haven't spent much time together. I miss you."

I smile. "I miss you too. Let's do some sisterly bonding."

Robin loops her arm through both of ours. She winces. "Sorry. Is it okay that I do this?" she asks me.

"I'm okay with it. I'd tell you if I wasn't."

We walk through stores with the hand-made hot cocoa from a cart. Robin buys plenty of clothes and accessories while I treat myself to a bobble of Shadow the Hedgehog and Bianca buys a fidget for stimming.

We run into familiar faces at the tiny arcade.

"Hey! How are you!" Alice squeals. She takes a sip of her smoothie.

Candace splashes herself with some of her smoothie upon seeing Bianca. "Oh, hey! I didn't see you there. I mean, now I do but…Well, how are you?" Her cheeks are redder than the Christmas bows.

Robin smirks at me as if to say I told you so. Even I can tell now that Candace likes Bianca. Bianca might feel the same because she stuffs her hands into her pockets before remembering one of her hands is holding a shopping bag. Her cheeks are just as red.

"Oh, nothing. Just walking around with Ellie and a, um, friend of Ellie's."

Alice raises a brow. "We know it's Robin. You don't have to worry. Your secret is safe with us."

Bianca isn't assured, though, based on her sharp inhale. I pat her on the shoulder. "Relax. Alice didn't rat out Robin when we snuck out to Doris's. We can trust them." I look at Alice. "We're treating Robin to the arcade. It turns out she loves arcades."

Robin plays it cool by shrugging. "And what if I do? I'm not just into mani-pedis, though they're godsends."

Alice nods. "For real. It's total bliss when you spend all day on your feet as a barista."

Candace straightens her back. "Would you like to hang out with us?" She looks at Bianca.

Bianca grins. "We'd love to. I mean, we'd like to. Sure."

They walk ahead of us to pay for coins. "You think they'll ask each other out?" I wonder.

Alice rolls her eyes. "Candace is fearless when it comes to helping Mom run the gift store and running volunteer activities but not flirting with girls. It'll take a Christmas miracle."

"Same with Bianca. Anyway, let's play."

The next hour flies as we play games from the racing ones to basketball, in which one bounces off the hoop and almost hits me. I win enough tickets from various games to get a stuffed orca.

"It'll be one of Mom's gifts. She loves whales," I say.

Robin strokes the stuffed octopus she won and laughs at our bemusement. "What? It's my favorite animal."

"I can't judge." Alice proudly holds up her poop emoji pillow.

We're standing to the side and notice Bianca approaching Candace with a stuffed elf. We move closer because we have no qualms about eavesdropping. They don't see us peering around one of the machines as Bianca spends a minute asking Candace out, to which Candace says yes.

Robin smiles. "Good for them. I'm having fun. Despite what people think, I'm capable of having fun."

I frown. "Don't listen to everyone. The archetype of a grumpy Christmas-hating person is problematic because the assumption is that nobody is allowed to be sad or angry during the holidays. It's okay not to be okay, and studies show that the holiday blues are real. I analyzed the trope on my blog."

"It's not surprising," Alice says. "My cousin has depression, and the holidays are hard because of the pressure to be cheerful. Ellie is right, Robin. Don't listen to people who tell you to act fine when you're not."

All she does is shrug before rejoining Candace and Bianca. Alice turns to me. "I hope she'll be okay."

"Me too."

CHAPTER 7

Holiday tradition: volunteering

Robin and I are hiding at the inn the next day.

Saturday mornings are meant for relaxation anyway, so neither of us minds too much. Jane thought it'd be best if Robin stayed inside until the excitement from the Mrs. Claus event cools down. Bianca feels I should stay out of sight, too, because she's gotten requests for an interview with the mystery elf.

The thrumming in my body and head won't stop as I imagine reporters tracking me down or people on my blog demanding to know more about me or Robin. My leg is bouncing until Robin holds it down.

"Even if they find you, why's it a big deal? Why do you hate attention so much?"

I wrap my arms around my legs. "I never get the good kind of attention. I've only gotten attention when I did something wrong, embarrassed myself, made someone mad, got teased, and so on. I don't have positive associations with attention."

"People knowing who you are could benefit your blog."

"I'm reminding myself. Thanks to you, I have fifty followers on my blog, and at least four hundred on each social media channel. Each post has more than five likes now. Thanks." I smile at her.

She waves a dismissive hand. "No sweat. I still can't believe that's the favor you asked me for."

I twist my hair. "I'm not good at anything else, thus dropping out of clubs. This is the one thing I'm good at and passionate about. I'm not sure about a lot except I want to be a media critic. Did you always want to be an actress?"

Her phone rings before she can answer. Her face drains of color seeing the caller ID. "I've got to take this." She slams the bathroom door shut behind her.

The door fails to keep the conversation private, at least on Robin's end. "I said I'd loan you a little. I'm not giving you more because you can't stay away from the casino." A pause. Robin growls frustratedly. "Do not call me a Grinch! I'm sick of people calling me that! And you do not get to call me cranky, you of all people!"

A loud thud makes me jump. "I'm not giving you a cent! Why can't you call me because you want to talk to your daughter?"

A scream makes me yank the door open. Robin is not hurt but she's huddled in the bathtub, hyperventilating. I kneel beside the tub.

"What do you need?" My hand hovers, unsure if I should touch her without permission. I wouldn't want someone to touch me without asking with the exception of

Bianca and Mom. I especially want to be sensitive given Robin's history of being harassed by men.

"Talk again. Please." She rocks back and forth.

I sit on the toilet while twisting my hands. I ramble about my favorite tropes (i.e., shrinking violet gaining confidence) and least favorites (girl getting a makeover to become desirable).

"I meant what I said at the arcade about the grumpy character during the holidays being problematic. The person on the phone shouldn't have called you that. This is a glass house situation because they call you grumpy, implying you have no goodwill or cheer yet that person wasn't spreading goodwill by calling you names. I tend to point out hypocrisy in my reviews."

A tearstained face is revealed when she lifts her head. "I never thought of it that way. I should point that out to her next time."

"Was that one of your parents?" I wince. "Sorry. I forget about boundaries sometimes."

"That was my mom. She's a mom in name only." She wipes snot with her arm. I hand her a tissue. "My parents never hit me but hurt me in other ways: criticizing everything, leaving me home alone for a few days at a time, inviting total strangers over for parties, passing out drunk. I won't bore you with the unabridged version. They pushed me into acting to get rich. Money has always been their true love."

She blows as loud as a horn into the tissue. "We didn't do the holidays. I tried giving them presents, but they never liked what I made or got them and told me to forget Christmas. I've never celebrated Christmas. One of my reasons all my exes are exes is that I refused to partake in the holidays. I never told them why because, as my therapist puts it, I try to keep people out."

"Then why do you tell me so much?"

She laughs in that way that isn't funny or happy. "Honestly, I don't have friends or reliable family members, so you're it besides my therapist and Jane. I'm sick of having no one. I'm even sicker of acting, especially after that recent movie where I played a porcupine who became human and had to find true love to stay human. Please don't ask." She laughs but it's hollow.

I cock my head. "Why not quit?"

She snorts. "My parents still need money most of the time. I've only ever known acting. I'm not great at anything else. I can empathize with you on that point."

"If your parents are terrible, why do you help them?"

"It doesn't take a psychologist to know that we love our parents even when they don't deserve it."

I help her stand and walk back to the bed. We sit in silence until I get a text from Bianca. "We have to be at the school in an hour. I can tell them you're sick."

"I'm good. I've gotten my act together before after panic attacks."

She wipes her eyes, opens her mouth, closes it, then opens it again as though she was debating where to say anything. "Thank you. I know you're just helping me for the blog and Bianca but thanks for being there for me."

"I don't try to help just to benefit myself. I don't like seeing people upset. Do you have trouble believing people can care about you? I gathered that based on what I've seen in characters like you in books and movies. You don't have to be guarded all the time."

She lets go of me with narrowed eyes as she backs away. "God, can you stop comparing everything to movies? I'm not some archetype you can analyze." She turns her back to me. "Whatever. Let's just go."

Why do I always mess things up? I mentally scold myself as I lead Robin to my car.

*

Madison Grove Elementary has not changed.

Not the old-fashioned red bricks, not the garden chairs and cement pots for plants that are covered in snow, not even white walls that are brightened up with winter crafts and drawings. Bianca squeezes my hand as she notices my determination to race through these halls; I don't need the stress ball. For example, the doors of the library, where I spent lunch alone each time a friendship expired. I take deep breaths as we pass a classroom where a teacher yelled at me for crying yet again for another bad grade.

Robin says nothing but sticks close to me like a guard. That somewhat soothes the agitation; only getting out of here will relieve me.

We reach the pinnacle of my nightmares: the cafeteria, often spent alone or with the next friend who pity-friended me or genuinely tried to be a friend until they lost patience. The tables are moved to the side and second graders sit in rows of chairs with teachers. I scan the little faces for anyone who looks isolated but my attention is snatched by the approaching principal.

"Welcome, Ms. Darcy! We're so excited to have you here!" Mrs. Jordan shakes Robin's hand so violently that Robin almost falls forward.

Robin dons her smile, her best accessory. "Thank you for having me. I'm surprised you recognized me. I'm mostly in TV movies and guest star in shows."

"That's still famous in my book, and I loved the TV movie you did about the daughter and mom running a pickle shop." My old principal's mouth opens upon noticing me. "Oh, hi, Ellie. How are you? It's been so long. You were one of my nicest students."

I never got why teachers always say that. "Why do people assume shy and quiet equals niceness? I could have been plotting world domination." She doesn't laugh with me.

Her smile wavers. "So, um, how are things? I've always been curious about how you're doing. I'm always scared for students like you who have so many struggles."

The temptation to be snarky is so strong until I remember how she didn't suspend me for shoving a bully and how she never made getting accommodations difficult. "I'm fine. In fact, I have a blog. But we should get this started."

"That's great, and you're right. Let's get started." Mrs. Jordan claps her hands. Everyone falls silent. "Hello, everyone! Thank you so much for being here and volunteering to pack bags for an emergency shelter."

"Our teachers made us," a boy points out. "You're not even really famous." This remark causes Robin to clench her jaw.

Mrs. Jordan purses her lips, choosing to ignore him. "We have a special guest today. Welcome TV actress Robin Darcy!"

The kids, especially girls, cry "Yay!" and wave their hands. Robin waves. "Hi, everyone. I'm sure some of you have seen my movies or TV shows."

"I loved your show about the girl who attends a school full of monsters and witches!" a girl cries out.

"Your holiday movies rock!" another calls out.

"You're, like, one of those people I've seen in a bunch of things but I didn't know your name until now," a boy says, earning a whispered scolding from a teacher.

Robin puts a hand to her chest. "Aww, thank you! You're all too sweet. What I like better than acting is giving back. After we pack the plastic bags, we're going to take a short video together. Your parents signed permission forms so you can be in it. In the video, I'm going to ask people to donate to the shelter and then post it. Let's make those packages so we can take that vid, okay?"

I've never seen kids quicker to get to work than now. The local reporter and another from a different town walk around to capture every angle of the workstations, which are long tables at which kids and Robin put mini water bottles, lip balm, mittens, socks, toothbrushes, toothpaste, and hand sanitizer into plastic bags.

Bianca has me stay to the side so I don't gain more attention as she keeps an eye on things. I'm to take Robin back to the inn when this is over whereas Bianca will meet with Jane. Otherwise, I have no purpose here.

I go to the Bio section of my blog. Robin said people like to connect, something I stink at. What if people make fun of me liking kid shows and cozy video games like people have in real life? What if they deem me boring like one boy called me on a play date for preferring to watch TV instead of playing outside?

No, I need to stop holding myself back. Bianca says it's not our job to make people comfortable. It's not just about my blog. I need to stop hiding myself. Robin deals with unwanted attention and opinions while handling panic attacks. I can do this.

The next hour is spent editing my Bio to include my love of hot chocolate, my hobbies like casual video games, reading, and watching TV, of course, and my identity as aroace and autistic. I add two pictures: one in which I hold a bobble of Invader Zim and another in which I'm dressed as Agatha Harkness for Halloween. My trembling finger hovers over the publish button for almost a minute before I finally hit it. As usual, I use an app to create a graphic to put on social media to share news.

My toes curl in my ankle boots as I anticipate the response, though people usually don't react for hours to posts. I whip my phone in and out of my pocket as I struggle with temptation to edit or delete.

Robin takes the video with the kids, asking people to donate money or supplies to the shelter. The kids proudly hold up their paper bags. One shouts they are famous after Robin finishes the video.

Mrs. Jordan poses for photos with Robin and the kids and teachers. Bianca is drinking from her travel mug when one of the kids knocks into her. She falls against Robin, who is drinking from her water bottle. They fall against the table, both bottle and mug spilling water and tea onto the plastic bags.

Bianca gasps, wringing her wrists at the destruction. Robin swears under her breath. Mrs. Jordan covers her mouth with her hand.

"Oh, no," she says. She addresses the kids. "Everything is okay. It was an accident." She sounds like she's trying to convince herself.

"We did that for nothing?" a boy groans.

"Will the people at the shelter not get these packs now?" another boy asks.

"Can't we just get more plastic bags?" Robin asks.

"The items weren't touched but the shelter won't risk anything even though the bags were zipped shut."

"I'm so sorry."

Bianca breathes heavily. I rub her back. "You've got to figure something out."

"I know!" she snaps. She closes her eyes, inhales sharply, then tells everyone, "What happened wasn't, um, great but not to worry. Everyone will appreciate the effort and it makes for a funny video. I'm sure the reporters caught everything." She looks slash glares at them.

"But now the people won't get stuff they need," a little girl says.

I whisper an idea into Robin's ear. She frowns but sees she has no better options. She says, "I'm happy to make a donation to the emergency shelter. It will cost whatever the total supplies for these kits cost. We could also share a message with the shelter from the kids. You can say anything you want as long as it's positive."

The kids light up at this idea. Some cheer. Mrs. Jordan nods. "We could retake the video you took, Robin, and whichever child wants to say something can do so. The permission forms should cover that."

Robin prepares another video. She says the same thing she did before except she says, "An unfortunate little accident happened. That teaches me not to drink water or tea near a table of donations." She shows the table behind her, still dripping tea and water onto the floor. "But I shall cover the costs of those donations because the kids worked really hard. They also want to share a special message with all of you."

At least ten kids say something positive about not giving up hope, hoping things get better, things like that.

Robin finishes by saying, "For those of you who want to help people going through rough times, you can volunteer and donate money but you can also find innovative ways to address these issues. You can find a nonprofit in this community, New Jersey, or something national that addresses things that lead to these issues, like unemployment or poverty."

The adults in the room look surprised. I'm proud of myself for coming up with this idea and proud of Robin for going along with it.

One of the kids glances my way then gasps, dramatically putting her hands on her face. "Hey! You're the elf that helped Mrs. Claus at the mall!"

I stop breathing when one of the camera people hears and turns our way. I turn away from him. "No, I'm not. I don't look like the elf."

"Yeah, you do! You even sound like her!"

Everyone turns our way. Everyone's gaze weighs on me like stones. A reporter blocks me on the way out.

"Is it true? Are you the mystery person seen with Robin Darcy?" He shoves his microphone in my face.

I push it away. "Uh, you almost took out my face with that." I open my mouth but stand there gaping like a fish as I consider my next steps. If Robin's experience has taught me anything, and my own experiences, it's that people will believe what they want to believe. I shouldn't have to be afraid of attention. "Yeah, I am."

Robin pulls me aside. "What are you doing?"

"I'm done being afraid of embarrassing myself. I could add being on the news and being brave to list of things I've tried that I've seen in movies." My smile is shaky. "Is that okay?"

She doesn't look like she agrees but she nods and turns us back toward the cameras. "This is Ellie. She's been showing me around town and attending to whatever I need when my manager's assistant can't."

Bianca joins us. "That's correct. Ellie volunteered to watch Robin when her manager Jane Keller and I handle other things like arranging these events. It's good to have someone close to your age with you when you're in a town you've never been to before."

Bianca drags us away. She takes me by the shoulders once we're outside. "Are you okay?"

I'm shaking so much I'm surprised I can still stand.

"I'm excited."

"Is your blog worth the exposure? People can be mean, especially if they find out you're autistic."

"Let them. I've dealt with bullies before."

"Then why are you squeezing your phone?"

I loosen my grip. "I can be nervous but confident at the same time. Trust me, Bianca. I'm just glad we were able to fix the situation."

She smiles. "That's right. Thank you so much. You're doing my job for me, first at the mall and now." She looks glumly at her feet. "I'm useless."

"No, you're not. Cut yourself some slack."

"Just take Robin back to the inn. I have to meet Jane somewhere." She walks away with hunched shoulders.

Once we're in my car, Robin says, "You're brilliant. You saved me again. You're good for more than just following me around."

I flip her off but smile. "I'm glad it worked out, though I'm worried about Bianca." I get a notification on my phone. "I got a reminder about something I've always wanted to try. Want to go to open mic? It's tonight."

"Why are you asking me? I thought I'd be the last person you'd want to go with."

"I, um, am fine doing things alone but not in crowded, loud places. Bianca is busy, and I don't have friends either. Please? You owe me for the ill-advised club fiasco."

She grimaces at the reminder. "Okay, but only because I'll be bored to tears in my room. You might have to disguise yourself."

I grin as I pull out of my spot. "Another thing that's on my list based on the spy movie genre."

Her shoulders shake as she laughs. "You'll get tired of disguises pretty quickly. But I'll let you live your fantasy."

I text Bianca to invite her along. She texts back she'll be too busy. I try not to let her hundredth promise to hang out soon spoil my excitement.

CHAPTER 8

Holiday tradition: listen to holiday music

The café is already full.

We get the last open booth by some holiday miracle. I fan my face with my hand; the hotness must be from the body heat from so many bodies. I'm surprised there is room for a space cleared in front of one of the walls for a microphone and speakers. The current performer is a violinist whose strings produce screeches rather than lovely notes. I cover my ears until it's over. Two people are polite enough to clap.

Robin removes my hands from my ears. "She's done. The next person is going up. I thought my ears were going to bleed. Loud noises bother you, right?"

I stir the cheese in my hot chocolate. I'm finally trying it after weeks of Doris insisting that I try it, and it's tasty. Doris says it was one of her favorite treats growing up in Puerto Rico before moving to New Jersey at the age of ten. "Yeah, but I won't have a meltdown anymore. I go outside when I need a break. That wasn't a matter of noise for me. That was a matter of terrible non-music."

Robin takes a bite out of her flan. "You can say that again. Thanks for coming. Emilio wasn't sure if you were really coming."

"Here I am. Wait a sec! You recognize us?" I look at the room to make sure nobody else recognizes me or Robin.

Alice rolls her eyes. "I won't rat you out. I recognized your voices and the way you walk. I'm a very observant person. I could be a detective."

When Alice walks away, Robin says, "Everything they have is so good. But that day you brought me here to cheer me up was a good day for me. Now I associate hot chocolate and this café with feeling safe and no longer viewing you as a forced presence in my life."

I chuckle. "Good to know." She doesn't need to know how a compliment like that warms my heart.

Emilio is behind the microphone, sitting on a chair with an acoustic guitar. He plays with a fidget spinner; he has never been self-conscious about stimming in public, which I envy. He reluctantly puts it in his pocket. His hands shake, microphone slipping in his hand. His voice shakes. "Hi, everyone. I'm Emilio, I work here, and this is my first time performing, so don't be too harsh."

"Is he the autistic worker? I hear it in his voice," I hear someone at the next table say.

My fist clenches around my stress ball. I peer around the wall separating our booth. "Does it matter if he is?"

The woman holds her hands up. "No need to get defensive. I was making an observation."

Robin pulls me back. "They're not worth it. Sit back, relax, and enjoy the music."

Emilio plays a few notes. I'm no musical expert but I can tell he's unsure and the notes are wrong. He stops, takes deep breaths and mutters under his breath, then continues. People whisper until they listen to the lively notes. Some customers clap to the classic song.

"He's great. Rocky start but it was his first time performing in public, I guess?" Robin asks.

"He said it was. He's talented. But I know he'll fixate on how he messed up. It's what he and I do."

"Well, someone should remind him to focus on how much he rocks. I messed up so many auditions when I started acting." She stares into her macchiato. "Sometimes I wish I had kept messing up so I wouldn't have become an actress. But then I remember the good times I've had during my career, and I remember all the people who *don't* suck, like Bianca and Jane. Jane is hard on the outside but soft inside like a chocolate turtle."

"If you weren't acting, what would you do?"

She doesn't answer. I think she's ignoring me until she pulls a pocket-sized lavender notebook out of her purse, the one she had out the other day. She holds it close like she's afraid I'll yank it from her.

"I dabble in writing ideas for movies and shows," she mumbles, then clears her throat. "It's silly stuff. I won't make a career out of it or anything."

"You said you write movie scripts?"

She opens her mouth, closes it. The next thing I know the notebook is shoved back into her purse. "Forget it. It's silly."

"Hey, don't say that. I get being nervous sharing stuff you made. I still get nervous writing blog posts."

"But it's harder to share stories!" Her cheeks flame. She looks around to see if anyone overheard. She lowers her voice. "I write short stories or ideas for shows. Did it since I was little. I made the mistake of sharing with my parents. They told me to stick to looking pretty."

"You know your parents stink, right?"

"I can know logically something but struggle to emotionally accept it."

I could push her but I wouldn't want someone to push me too hard about my blog. I've never talked about it except with Mom, Bianca, and Alice, and only because Alice brought it up. Past experience also tells me that Robin will snap if I push.

An obnoxious laugh makes us cringe. I stiffen upon seeing Hilary with two girls.

So much for being too busy with homework this weekend.

Hilary frowns upon locking eyes with me. She swiftly turns away, whispering something to her friends. They glance at me with chuckles.

I stand, knowing I'll beat myself up for it later but rage overcomes embarrassment. The stress ball acts like an emotional anchor in my hand so I don't fall apart from fear of confrontation or the hurt. I tap Hilary on the shoulder. My fists are clenched. "You said you were too busy this weekend. You didn't have to lie."

One of the girls gives me an "ugh" look. "She's allowed to have plans open up. Or if she didn't want to hang out with you, be happy she was too polite to hurt your feelings."

"I'm not talking to you. I'm talking to Hilary."

Hilary glares at me. "You had to know I was full of crap. You're not exactly the type of person someone hangs out with for fun. You get stressed by, like, everything, and clutch things like that ball." She points at it.

I blink back tears. I feel like an overheated teapot. "And you were so much fun at lunch?" I snap. Hilary's eyes dart around the room as heads turn. I don't care for once. "You know what? I'm glad this happened. Enjoy your tea. By the way, I noticed you because you laugh like a hyena. You say I'm irritating but you should look at yourself."

I point to her phone. "I noticed you looking up movies to see together. Funny how you turned down offers to watch movies at lunch but whatever. You should know people have been saying that movie is full of racist stereotypes and the ending has been leaked."

Her friends gasp. "Don't spoil the movie for us!" one of Hilary's friends whines.

"I would never. That's too evil. But I want to be a better person than you by warning you, even though you never appreciated my love of movies. Good night."

I return to the table. Robin hands me a napkin to wipe my eyes. I'm shaking. "She's not worth being upset over," Robin tells me.

"I don't care about her. We were never really friends. I'm just embarrassed that I thought we could become friends, that anyone would want to be friends with me. This is why I stopped trying to socialize." I turn toward the wall, hoping none of the other patrons are looking at me.

Robin leans toward me. "She's obviously the kind of person who doesn't appreciate a good friend."

I sigh. "I'm used to being overlooked. I'm just a nobody with a blog people only care about because you talked about it."

"People wouldn't keep following you if that were the case. In fact, you're brave for sharing your thoughts and being authentic. Maybe it's time I tried it."

Robin takes the notebook back out. She slides it across the table. "Read, before I change my mind."

The first few pages are ideas in bullet points regarding a potential show about a bisexual teen actress pressured by the industry and family to stay in the closet. There are details like character names, demographics for each character, a list of themes such as found family, and the setting would be in California where the main character lives and is filming a kids' TV show.

I look up at Robin. "We need more shows like this. This is awesome."

She plays with the spoon in her cup. "It's okay."

"Stop selling yourself short. You need to share this with people."

"First, I'd need to polish things up. I can't just submit bullet points."

"Then take classes."

"Can you stop giving me unsolicited advice?" At my hurt look, she softens. "I appreciate your compliments but I can't quit acting. At least not yet. Besides, it's only fair that you get out of your comfort zone if I'm getting out of mine."

I narrow my eyes at her. "Seriously? I put myself in the public spotlight today! How can I get any more uncomfortable than that? I also wore that uncomfortable elf costume to a club I didn't want to go to, a costume that gave me a serious wedgie, by the way."

I stare at the table. "I told you, I stink at jobs and clubs. I quit before they could fire me at the last job because I make people uncomfortable even when I'm super fake nice like other girls. I've tried. Trying isn't enough." I'm crying again.

"I get that. But I'm sure there's a job or a club that's the right fit for you."

Everything is too much. Memories of impatient bosses, clique-ish colleagues or club members, and displeased customers cause throat-burning bile to rise in my throat. My fingers shake as I accept another napkin.

"I need to go outside a minute." I rush outside, where I lean against the wall and embrace the cool air against my hot, sweaty skin.

The cool air and space soothe the burning sensation that comes with unwanted memories. I no longer feel trapped. I know people saw me cry and rush past them, so knowing they can no longer see me also relaxes me. It also gives me incentive to stay outside so I don't' have to face their pity.

Although shame no longer floods my body, heated anger lingers that makes my skin itch. I gnash my teeth at the idea of facing Robin again. She accuses me of hypocrisy but she just gave me unsolicited advice. Is she that different from other people who've told me how to exist? From people who tell me to keep trying and insist they understand but they don't?

The door to the café opens. Robin lingers in the doorway before tentatively joining me.

"I'm sorry. I realized I told you not to give me advice but I did the same thing."

I focus on the street, on the way the patches of ice in the street and on the lampposts glitter in the streetlights. Studying the number of discarded coffee cups and napkins prevents me from crying or snapping.

"Can you talk to me?"

I stare at the stuffed animals lining the rear window of someone's car as though their fake eyes can support me. "You said you get what I'm going through, but you don't. You don't know what it's like to be autistic or anxious. That's like me saying I get what you go through as an actress."

"You're right. I don't get it. Come back inside before you become the next episode of a true crime show. If something happens to you, Jane might stick me with a real bodyguard, someone who's more of a stickler for the rules than you." She smiles but grimaces when I don't laugh with her.

"I need a few more minutes. Is it okay if we don't talk? I like to focus on random things to calm down."

"Sure. Silence is underrated."

The silence of the street is punctured by blaring holiday music from a family-filled car as well as a group of teens walking by with flasks. Otherwise, the scene is right out of a holiday card: snow-capped potted bushes and streetlights, holiday decorations in every window, and the thin trees on the sidewalks wrapped in white lights. The only other business open at this time is the diner. I watch two women kiss and fawn over their baby at their spot in the window. Waitresses in the background constantly flash by with coffee pots and trays.

"It's fun to watch people," Robin says.

"Do you think any of them fake holiday happiness?" I wonder.

"Oh, yeah. Everyone does. It's just that I'm the perfect scapegoat for grumpiness. Maybe I should write a movie addressing this topic."

"I would watch that movie. I watch people sometimes to try to picture what it'd be like with a dad. He walked out on me when I was little after I was diagnosed with autism. Bianca told me he couldn't handle another autistic daughter. I don't really miss the guy because I don't remember him but I still wonder what might have been. It doesn't take a psychology degree to figure out that my daddy issues are part of the reason I hesitate to trust people. Hooray for self-awareness."

She snorts. "You and me both. Maybe that's one of the reasons it's not a *total* bummer being stuck with you." She scratches her head. "God, this wig is itchy."

She tugs on it. "Don't take it off!" I say.

"Just a minute. There's nobody around." She takes it off, sighing in relief. She takes off her sunglasses.

I freeze when someone at a table inside looks out the window. We are inches apart with only the glass between us, meaning this woman gets a really close look at Robin's face.

She jumps up and points at Robin. We jump back when she bangs on the glass.

Other café patrons look our way. Robin has put her wig and sunglasses back on. But it's too late. I think I saw someone take a picture.

We make a break for it. Doris pushes through the crowd with Emilio. I shout back, "Great job!"

"Thanks!" he shouts back. "Run like the wind!"

We turn the corner and hide in an alley until we're sure the coast is clear. Robin can't stop laughing.

"Oh, god. Bianca is going to be pissed. I already messed up today." I push my back against the wall, something I sometimes do during stress.

"It's fine. Even if someone took a picture, so what? I don't think open mics are scandalous."

That's true. My heart races a little less. "Let's get out of here. I hope you had fun."

"I did. Thanks, Ellie." She swears when she steps in a suspicious-looking brown puddle. "Seriously? These are new boots! Is this the price to pay for escaping unwanted attention?"

I laugh and eventually Robin joins me, though she keeps looking mournfully at her boot.

Who would have thought I'd be out past nine thirty at night walking to my car to escort a celebrity back to the inn? Even more astounding is the fact I'm becoming friends with a famous person if we aren't already.

No, I should watch myself. Robin could be being polite when she says she likes me. Politeness is instinctual. I've tricked myself into believing people genuinely like me before. When will I learn?

CHAPTER 9

Holiday tradition: Mom making me hot chocolate

School is unbearable, and that's really saying something given my experience.

Normally, I get attention for meltdowns, saying the wrong thing, or "walking like a penguin" as people put it. Now I'm stared at for being associated with Robin. At least I'm already used to staring at the ground so I don't have to meet anyone's eyes or see them snapping photos.

Not that literally keeping my head down prevents people from bothering me. Teens are basically unpaid paparazzi who are already experts at throwing questions at me, feeling entitled to answers, and asking me what my problem is when I don't respond.

The last straw is at lunch when a guy shoves his phone in my face, hitting my nose without so much as an apology. "Were you really at open mic with Robin Darcy? Did she perform?"

"Can everyone back off?" I shout. The cafeteria goes quiet.

I should walk away. But I'm done cowering. I'm also at the boiling teapot state, where I'm so hot I can't contain what comes out of me.

The rage inside me is like a hungry scorpion spreading its poison through me, demanding more sustenance. "You're all so pathetic by obsessing over famous people, judging them but wanting attention from them at the same time. You're hypocrites! And you ignore me when I'm not embarrassing myself, so why should I give any of you the time of day?"

I storm out of the cafeteria with speed that would make my physical education teacher proud. My foot pays for my anger when I kick the wall next to a set of lockers. All I can hear is my breathing and the echoes of my shoes in the hall as I pace. It is amazing my stress ball endures my iron-clad grip.

I jump when I see Alice. She approaches me like I'm an agitated dog. "I saw what happened. I wanted to check on you. It'd be pointless to ask if you're okay."

I turn from her. I can't stand when people see me like this. "I will be okay. Thanks for checking on me."

"What you did was cool, telling everyone off. I have to say, it's been great seeing you speak up more. I sometimes felt like you didn't want to be bothered, whether it was here or at the café. Nicole always wondered, too, why you act distant."

"I'm sorry. It's not you. I just always fear saying the wrong thing, though I obviously still make people uncomfortable by staying quiet. I didn't mean to make you or Nicole feel like I don't like you."

She digests my words, then says, "I'm here if you ever want to talk or want to sit with me at lunch."

Great. The millionth pity lunch invite of my life. She must be a mind reader because she holds up a hand before I speak. "I'm not offering out of pity. I think you're cool. Plus, you can test out ideas I have for the café menu. I've been experimenting with cookie recipes. Want to try a gingerbread slash peppermint cookie I made?"

That sounds like a little much especially given I don't like gingerbread, but this may be the first time someone's lunch invite is sincere. My shoulders relax and my hand loosens on the stress ball.

"I can run blog post ideas on you in return. If you don't mind."

"Fair trade, especially if my cookies make you want to hurl."

"Oh, dear." But I laugh as we reenter the cafeteria. My and Alice's glares inspire people to lower their phones or at least be less obvious. Alice's contraption makes my stomach upset but it's worth chatting about my blog, meeting Alice's three equally cool and equally nice friends, including Nicole, and enjoying lunch period for the first time in years. At least Alice's art is better than her baking as I see when she shows me preliminary sketches and designs for stickers, watercolor portraits, and wall decals.

Hilary avoids my eyes at another table. In the past, I would have been stung that she didn't stick up for me. But the truth is that we were just people who sat together to avoid looking like losers who sit alone at lunch. But now I have someone who actually seems interested in the stuff I say and gives me feedback on blog ideas. Even her friends share their opinions.

Before lunch ends, Alice says, "The café is hiring if you need a job. It might be cool to work together."

"Or you could volunteer at the library," Nicole says. "Think of all the books. Our coffee is nothing to rave about but at least it'll be free."

My heart falls into my stomach. "Maybe." I think of the messed-up orders, forgotten tasks, or accidental insulting of customers like when I said, "I don't know because I haven't been here all day," which in hindsight I know sounds rude but I literally meant I hadn't been at work until the afternoon so I couldn't answer a question.

Mom loves the idea when I tell her once I'm home. Robin is with Bianca and Jane right now, so I'm off-duty. "I'll just screw up," I tell Mom as we munch on sugar cookies in the living room while watching *Klaus,* my next movie to review.

She pauses the movie. "I'll pause because I know you like to be focused for movies you review. Think about the job. Doris is super patient and she'll give you accommodations. Did you ask your former employers for accommodations? Wait, I shouldn't ask. Sorry if I'm being nosy."

"No, it's fine. I asked them to repeat them and asked questions whenever I wasn't sure but I didn't ask for things like written instructions. I felt like I wouldn't get hired if I asked."

"Well, see what happens next time you interview for a job. If they don't like it, it's not the job for you."

"Easy for you to say. You don't have my struggles. Everyone loves you. Even dad loved you, didn't he? He left because of me and Bianca, not you." I swallow a lump in my suddenly dry throat. My eyes sting like they do every time I think about the reason dad left, and probably why other people don't stick around too long.

She grabs my shoulders. "Stop right there. He left because he was a poor excuse of a human being. For the thousandth time, him leaving was his fault, not yours. I've done my best to make sure he didn't ruin your self-esteem."

"It's not just him. Other people get impatient with me when I mess up, and I can't blame them."

"Honey, not everyone thinks like the jerks who have hurt you or underestimated you. I know you'll do great at something you enjoy and where people see your value. You're good at watching Robin. However, I did hear a rumor that you two attended open mic night when you told me you were at the inn. Is that true?" She crosses her arms.

I fidget. "Okay, fine. I'm sorry."

She smiles. "I should be mad but I'm glad. You hardly ever go out. Robin couldn't have a better person keeping her out of trouble."

She wouldn't say that if she knew I took Robin to a club. She turns the movie back on. I can't focus on it and resolve to rewatch it later.

The idea of applying for a job, let alone working one, sounds as appealing as walking in the cold in a tank top and shorts but Mom has a point. If anyone would be patient, it's Doris. Emilio would be patient, too, because he gets the struggles of working while neurodivergent.

Besides, the blog and my social media are getting ever more popular, though the DMs I've gotten are overwhelming and not related to my reviews. Many want to know what it's like to know Robin and if I can introduce them to her. I've had to delete quite a few gross messages from guys.

Mom sees me doing this and takes my phone. "You're taking a break." She puts it behind her back.

"Come on!"

"You're not looking at any more messages."

I rub my head. "What sucks is they don't care about my content. I wonder if people will unfollow when they realize I won't introduce them to Robin."

"It'll be okay. That's what I always say."

"I'm allowed to wallow in self-pity."

"That's true, but try to relax. I know it's not easy but try. I can make you Italian hot chocolate."

My mouth waters with anticipation of the thickness and creaminess that is more delicious than weak instant packets. I get mugs from the cabinet even though we still have to actually make the hot chocolate.

Her mugs are always unique with sayings that aren't appropriate for children, not that that stopped her from sharing those mugs with us as children. They never fail to inspire or make me smile, including this one. It says "Someone who says you're too much is jealous."

Mom gestures to it. "You make fun of my fondness for quotes."

"You put quotes everywhere in the house and on your shirts." I look at the shirt that declares she is a boss lady then at her oversized beaded earrings. "To be serious, you're unique and I love you for it. I loved that you didn't care about fitting in."

"I learned long ago that trying to be something I'm not won't do anything. Sometimes it does gain you friends but not friends who stand by you. I know you've figured that out. I can't stand the pressure to fit unrealistic standards for mothers like volunteering at every event. There's no time and I'm already involved in your life."

She taps her finger on the counter. "You know my childhood is why I was determined to be a good mom to you and your sister and why I stay true to who I am. My parents were rich snobs who wanted to mold me into an obedient puppet. Your grandfather tended to forget his humble origins as a poor Italian immigrant and was all about assimilation except for language and food, of course. I'm amazed your grandfather kept me in the will after I cut them off."

We tried having a relationship with my grandparents. However, Grandma felt Mom coddled me and Grandpa was as silent and distant as a mountain. They constantly belittled Mom's craft shop and masseuse job, saying she could've been a lawyer or accountant. The final straw was when I overheard a fight between them in which they blamed Mom for Dad walking out for "catering to" me and Bianca, and told her how shameful divorce is. He alternated between Italian and English, and I understand enough Italian to have gotten the gist. She told them what they could do with themselves and cut them off.

"You haven't had good experience with attention but you deserve to shine, sweetie."

I don't want to ruin this moment by telling her she's wrong so I'm silent.

Bianca enters the living room and hops on the couch, putting me in the middle. Her knee bounces until I stop it with my hand.

"How was your date with Candace?" I ask.

She grins. "Awkard at first but that's par for the course with me. And with her. Then we couldn't stop talking. We both love romance books, the same shows, hate alcohol, and love the same cute animal videos. It's like we were meant to be."

"That's great, honey," Mom says. "And how is work?"

"For once, I feel confident. I haven't gotten anything wrong. Jane even told me I'm doing a good job." She squeals. "Things are finally going well. I don't think I would've gotten this opportunity to prove myself if not for Robin. I should thank her."

"I told you things would work out. I was just telling your sister that."

I roll my eyes as Mom relays the job opening at the café. Bianca tells me, "It's up to you. You've done lots of bold things lately, so I would think working at a café with a woman who would definitely accommodate you would be the least scary thing you've done."

That's true. I helped Robin at the mall. I told the world I'm the one who has been keeping an eye on Robin when I hate the spotlight. I stood up to everyone at school. I stood up to Hilary.

I text Alice, who gave me her number, to say I'd be interested in applying for the job.

CHAPTER 10

Holiday tradition: get holiday books from library

This may be the first time I've never wanted to be at the library.

It may be blasphemous to even think since I usually get a rush coming here to check out books and get a one-dollar hot chocolate (yes, I know I drink way too much hot chocolate). But I'm here against my will today, something I never thought I would think. The two-story, brown-brick library is fuller than normal thanks to people who want to get a glimpse of Robin. The library security guards are more alert than usual, having barred more people, including reporters, from entering because the building is at capacity.

Not even getting two holiday books, one YA and one adult, eases my nerves as I wait with Robin to read to a group of first graders in the children's section. The librarians ushered us into the staff room, where we'll wait for Nicole to get us. She grinned on seeing me.

"Hey! Good to see you. This may be the first time you've volunteered here. But you have way more excitement than I normally do. I've never gotten to work with an actress!" She turns to Robin. "It's great to have you here. I like your movies, so today combines my love of books with love of your movies."

"Glad to hear it," Robin says.

Nicole goes out to finish prep.

We munch on muffins at the tiny table as we wait for Nicole to come back.

"A statue talks more than you do. Are you that nervous? I can tell Jane you got food poisoning or something," Robin offers. She wrinkles her nose at the muffin and tosses it into the trash. "It might not be a complete lie. These things are stale."

I squeeze the stress ball. "No, I'm just hopelessly awkward around people my age. I can do it. I want to be less shy. I even applied for a job even though I still have nightmares from my previous jobs."

She smiles. "That's great. But I can't believe Jane is doing this. No, wait, I can. Everyone is curious about you and what exactly you do for me, so she wants to milk it. She told me that being associated with you, a quiet small-town girl, will make me even more likeable. It's not fair to you."

"Life's not fair. I'm used to being used. I'm the person people rely on for group projects. Apparently, I'm the go-to for watching over stubborn celebrities."

Robin raises a brow. "How kind of you to say. I'll be sure to give you a five-star review so other celebrities can be graced with your presence."

People often think I don't understand sarcasm. That could not be more untrue. "How kind of you."

Nicole opens the door, pushing her curly black hair out of her face. "We're ready! I picked really great books all the kids love even if they' a little…odd." She glances at the crowd outside. "For what it's worth, I never agreed with all the crap they were saying about you," she tells Robin. "I don't think you should have to win people over but I hope things work out for you."

Robin smiles. "Thank you. That means a lot."

Nicole turns to me. "And I love your blog! Alice sent me the link the day we ran into each other. I get excited when I meet other bloggers. I have a blog that focuses mostly on disabled and neurodivergent Black fiction because we're still underrepresented. I have dyscalculia. Would you be open to suggestions on what to watch or read?"

"Absolutely!" Will I ever stop feeling like I'll float from joy whenever someone compliments the blog? "And I'd like to follow your blog."

"That'd be great. I'm glad we're talking. You never talk when I check out your books." She sees my wince. "Sorry. I'm not trying to make you feel bad. It's just you have so much to say on your blog that it'd be nice to hear what you have to say in real life."

"I'll try talking more, if it doesn't interrupt your work. I can give you reading recs then. And I think we have History together. I could share recs then, too, if you don't want to listen to the lesson."

"Yes, please!"

We brace ourselves and follow her. Parents, guardians, onlookers, and reporters surround us in a semicircle as we take two bean bags on the rough gray carpet that is brightened up with a rug made to look like a town. Stuffed snowmen peek from bookshelves at us as we take the books that Sofia hands to us.

Robin speaks to the cameras. "Hi, I'm Robin Darcy, and this is Ellie, who is kind of an assistant to me. She and I are going to be reading stories today."

Robin reads first from a book about a talking piece of holiday fungus who saves Christmas. Robin struggles to keep a straight face, as do I. Then again, I heard there was a story about holiday poop, so nothing should surprise me.

My book is just as, well, unique, to say the least. My main character is a holiday garden gnome who rescues other gnomes from a neighbor who doesn't like the holidays or garden gnomes.

"Your voice sounds weird and that ball is weird," a boy says, earning a nudge from his babysitter.

I stumble, embarrassed, but continue. You think I'd be used to people pointing out my stress ball, "autistic accent" or other things people perceive as flaws.

"Maybe but does it matter as long as you understand me? People can look, sound, or be different and that's a great thing. It's okay to use a stress ball like this to feel calm." I hold it up for everyone to see.

The boy sheepishly stays quiet the rest of the time. Nicole gives me a thumbs-up while Robin smirks.

The kids clap when we finish. I pose for photos with Robin and we head outside, where we are stopped by George

Thomas. "Those were some nice stories. So, Robin, you introduced Ellie as a type of assistant. What do you mean by that?"

Robin looks to me, probably as annoyed as I am that he's ignoring me like I'm a child. It's on principle that I speak up. "You can just ask me." I realize too late that I probably shouldn't be so curt on live TV.

He chuckles. "Sorry. I didn't mean to be rude. So, Ellie, what do you do for Robin? I assume you do more than coffee runs. You've gotten Robin out of some sticky situations."

I squeeze my phone inside my pocket. "Those situations were unfortunate but nobody's fault."

"Even the cookie fight?" He raises a brow.

My cheeks flush. "It was immature but ultimately harmless. It showed Robin's fun side when everyone was accusing her of being incapable of it," I say pointedly. "My sister, Bianca, handles the real stuff like preparing Robin for interviews and stuff. I show Robin around time when she has free time and help her de-stress, especially when she feels like she's alone. I don't have many people like that, so I understand."

"Is it because you're autistic?"

I feel like I plummeted from the sky and my heart is in my throat. Robin says, "Whoa, whoa, whoa."

I hold up a hand. "It's fine. Yeah, I am, and, yes, that's part of the reason. You could say Robin helped me out of my comfort zone."

Robin straightens her shoulders. "And Ellie has helped me step outside mine by coming to a small town and doing holiday activities I've never done before. I've never had a normal Christmas."

She looks at me. I try to convey that I'm here for her no matter what she chooses to disclose. She takes a deep breath. "I didn't have the best childhood, so that's one of the reasons I'm not a holiday person. But I've discovered the Christmas spirit, thanks to this town and thanks to Ellie, who has also helped me with panic attacks, something I haven't revealed before."

The reporters nearby whisper. George asks, "Have you struggled with panic attacks for a long time?"

"Yeah, I have. Since I was little. I used to be ashamed but I want to be more open. Now, if you'll excuse me."

Bianca helps us get away to her car. She says as she drives, "That was good, though off-script. But I can't promise Jane won't be annoyed at best, angry at worst. She said you won't get taken seriously as a woman in this industry by talking about your panic attacks."

"I'm done making other people comfortable. You can tell Jane I said that."

"However Jane feels, I'm proud of both of you. Ellie, you've become more confident lately."

I hold on to this warm, fuzzy feeling for dear life.

*

It has been a few hours since Bianca dropped us off at the inn.

We stand at attention like soldiers for an angry general when there is a knock at Robin's door. Robin tells her to come in then whispers, "It was nice knowing you."

Jane's face is as impassive as the mountains in the painting on the wall above Robin's bed. She turns from the frozen water to coolly regard us. Bianca stares into her tablet like she's hoping she'll get sucked into it. I look at my boots. I see Robin meeting Jane's gaze out of the corner of my eye.

I break the silence by saying, "Will you please say something?" Bianca nudges me again.

"Well, I saw the news and I wasn't pleased…at first. This could be a good thing."

I look up. "For real?"

Jane grins. "Bianca looked at social media and saw that many people think it's 'inspirational' that Robin shared her story. Lots of young people feel less alone for having panic attacks or less than ideal childhoods. Blogs and newspapers rave about this as well as Robin's friendship with you. They think you're inspirational, too."

Bianca acknowledges my existence for the first time in hours to share a pained look. "Am I inspirational just for being autistic? That's not okay if that's the case," I say.

Jane ignores me. "A really popular blog wrote an article about how people have been too hard on Robin and you were right to call people out. I think we can milk this even further." She turns to Robin with a gaze as hungry as a hawk's. "What if you told people how you've helped Ellie."

"With her blog?"

"Well, that, and in other ways. People eat up stories of celebrities helping disabled people."

I wouldn't be more taken aback if a polar bear stormed into the room. I feel a vein throb in my forehead. "What the hell?"

Jane cocks her head. "What's wrong?"

For once, Bianca doesn't shrink from Jane. She shakes her head at her boss slash mentor. "Jane, that's not okay! You also shouldn't lie. Robin hasn't done anything for Ellie besides help expose her blog."

Her boss shrugs. "Sometimes our job involves stretching the truth. And maybe you don't have to see this as inspiration porn." She turns to me with a grin and dares to use the tone people use with me like I'm a child. "Wouldn't you like to be famous? If you're serious about being a film critic, it could help being connected to a famous face."

I'm so angry I'm not even tempted. "Don't use the baby voice with me. What would you have Robin lie about anyway?"

Jane taps her chin. "Hmm…We could say Robin has helped you get out of the house more, talk to more people, and stuff like that."

"I'm not a hermit! I don't have dozens of friends but I do stuff and I talk to people, just not all the time!"

Robin throws her arms up. "I guess you're also going to have me do some kind of mental health campaign despite all the times you told me to hide it? Talk about hypocrisy."

"I only said that for fear nobody would work with you. There is still such a stigma. I was protecting you."

"You were keeping the status quo. Screw you. Come on, Ellie. I'm done."

Robin holds the door open for me. I look at Bianca.

She won't even look at me. I swallow a lump in my throat and

follow Robin.

CHAPTER 11

Holiday tradition: holiday activities at the park

Madison Grove Park is full of life.

The park transforms into a winter wonderland that glows with white light from the holiday lights and streetlamps. Stalls and pop-up tents entice visitors with potential Christmas gifts as well as irresistible aromas of cinnamon, nutmeg, sugar, peppermint, and chocolate from beverages and treats. Robin and I gave in to temptation by buying cinnamon-sprinkled hot chocolates that we nurse between gloved hands as we walk.

"It's unhealthy how much hot chocolate we've been drinking but I'm too sad to care," I remark.

"I have noticed you drink a lot of it. It seems to be more than just a sweet tooth."

I ponder before answering. "Hot chocolate brings comfort, not just to me but the world. Hot chocolate is a symbol of comfort and love. It's what moms or close family members offer when someone is sad and it's one of the things people look forward to in winter. That's why people think cozy living rooms and family time when they think hot chocolate. I drink it when I have a bad day, even in spring and summer."

I stir my hot chocolate before adding, "Comfort is big to me. It's why I stay home, because no one can hurt me and I can't mess things up as much. I feel like a hypocrite sometimes when I try new things for my blog because I try little things like taking a salsa class, which I stink at. But I don't try the really major stuff like trying to make new friends or asking people to collaborate on my blog."

She seems to analyze my answer. She stares into her hot chocolate. "Whenever I imagined the type of holiday I always wanted, I pictured my mom making me hot chocolate and watching a movie together. And you taking me to Doris's Café after the cookie fight to make me feel better is part of why I began trusting you. For what it's worth, you've been taking a lot of huge risks, lately. You've grown. I wish I could."

"Who says you haven't?" She doesn't respond to that but her lips twitch like she's holding back a smile.

We sit on one of the benches, beating a couple who give us dirty looks. Robin glares so hard they scurry away.

"I'm over everything: trying to fix my image, being who people want me to be, which includes being jolly when I'm just not."

She sees me shaking and takes my cup when I'm in danger of dropping it. I squeeze the bench. "I've never been so far out of my comfort zone before. I don't usually do a lot. I've had so much autistic burnout that I need fuzzy slippers, a video game, a nap, and/or to wrap myself in my blankets when I get home."

"Autistic burnout is from socializing or doing a lot, right?" She shrugs when my eyes widen. "I did research. I'm sorry you're going through that. I didn't want a babysitter, yet now I'm sad at the idea of you quitting. If Jane doesn't fire you first."

I flinch with a roiling stomach. "It wouldn't be the first time a boss didn't like me. I was so scared about disappointing her and Bianca, and that's exactly what happened today."

"We did nothing wrong."

For once, the terror of disappointing people vanishes. It is replaced by anger that is not hot but as cold and steely as the metal of the miniature rides at the park. I feel my eyes blaze with determination as I face Robin, who seems taken aback.

"People-pleasing has gotten me nowhere. My best was never enough at my jobs or the school clubs, with people I thought were friends, and it wasn't enough with Jane and

Bianca. I can't control what strangers think of my blog. I'm just over it."

"You know what? So am I. I'm done with this career and being something I'm not." Robin stands and plants her hands on her hips.

I laugh as I stand. "You should tell Jane. I'd love to see her face. You should also tell the world."

Her face lights up brighter than the lights. "Oh, my god. Yes! That's it! I have an idea. Follow me."

My gut tells me, "Oh, no." Excitement drowns it out as I watch Robin stand on the bench. She yanks off her wig and sunglasses. My fingers twitch as I follow suit, my gut screaming at me to go back to hiding as all eyes land on us. Phones are whipped out and people crowd around us.

Robin motions for me to come up. With shaking legs, I do, Robin having to catch me as I stumble. I want to curl into myself with all these eyes and flashing phones.

"Listen up, everyone!" Robin shouts. "I'm Robin Darcy and I have an important message to share, me and my friend."

She pauses, probably wondering if she made a mistake but she steels herself. "Film this because I have a message. You probably saw news about what I said this morning about having panic attacks and things about my past. I stand by everything. I also need to speak up on the cause of my public image makeover."

She gulps, probably remembering the horrible incident. "That Santa I shoved was harassing me. I wanted him to leave me alone. Nobody wanted me to talk about it but I'm talking now. I also felt nobody would believe me due to my reputation for being cold and mean. But I've pushed people away and partied hard to deal with past trauma and the trauma of being in this industry, honestly. I'm sorry about ruining that fair but not about pushing him. Part of my trauma includes emotionally abusive exes who used me but tried to dim my light at the same time."

Whispers spread like fire.

"I've been called hard to work with. That's only because I've suggested ways to improve a script or I called out costars or staff for inappropriate behavior. I hated attending functions because I get nervous in crowds and I hate the judgment, and partying a little too hard was a way of trying to cope. It doesn't help that many people who were supposed to be on my side told me to hide my panic attacks."

The crowd gets bigger. Robin pulls me toward her. "I couldn't have dealt with everything if not for this girl right here. She was hired to make sure I didn't get into trouble, basically a babysitter because my own manager didn't trust me not to cause trouble."

I can feel my hot chocolate threatening to come back up. I swallow the bile and scramble for words. My voice croaks so I have to repeat myself. "I'm Ellie and what Robin said is true. I have a blog called *Ellie's Film and TV Reviews.* Promoting my blog was the main reason I agreed to be Robin's babysitter as she put it. But I've also gained confidence and a real friend. I used to hide at home and behind my laptop because I came to be embarrassed of myself because so many people taught me to think that way since I was little.

Not anymore. If you talk about me and Robin, please don't say things like how 'inspirational' I am just for existing or how great Robin is for being friends with 'someone like me' because I'm autistic." I use air quotes. "I'm just a person like anyone else."

"That's right! And guess what? I'm writing show and movie scripts. That's my passion! Good night, everyone."

We push through the crowd after hopping off the bench. My heart roars in my ears as some people grab at us until kind security guards assist. Robin is green and keeps her head down, a stark contrast to our heads held high before. That makes me as nauseous as the entitlement people have for touching us, total strangers.

The guards get us to the parking lot. The tall, muscular one asks, "Are you okay? Don't celebrities usually have bodyguards?"

"My manager thought it'd be fine. She said I'm not famous enough for security threats, which somewhat hurts my ego. But people in a small town are excited about any celeb visiting. I'm going to educate her once I see her, don't worry," Robin says.

His partner, a woman with a crew cut, touches my shoulder. I stiffen, not liking just anyone touching me and especially hating pity touches. "Are you okay? You're shaking."

"I just need to calm down. Thank you."

We're left alone and we get into my car. Robin allows me to just sit and study our surroundings to ground myself. The glow, aromas, and sounds of the park are fainter under the sound of my running car. Squirrels and birds take advantage of the popcorn and other snacks littering the ground. The parking lot is dark despite the streetlamps, gloomy compared to the light of the park.

"I'm sorry you went through that. I can never get used to it, though to be fair, I don't go through it too much because I'm not an A-lister." Robin frowns when I don't chuckle with her. "Feeling better?"

"Yeah, I'm good. I'm anxious but also excited. It's like I drank four coffees." I take out the stress ball.

"I won't lie: we'll get in trouble. But relax! It was worth it. I think we did the right thing."

"I hate thinking of the consequences, so I'll focus on the rush I feel." The humming throughout my body will not stop. I embrace it.

Both our phones won't stop dinging. I see notifications from my blog and social media as well as a million texts from Mom and Bianca. I've been tagged in videos that were taken of us.

Robin smirks. "Jane can complain all she wants but the floodgates have opened." She looks at my phone. "Are you going to be okay? You don't like attention."

"I'm still nervous but excited. I chose to bring attention to myself. I regret nothing."

Here is hoping I still mean those words later. But for now, I relish the thrill of tonight as we leave the parking lot. Robin plays girl-power songs that we sing (off-key) to. I let her squeeze my stress ball.

CHAPTER 12

Holiday tradition: making ricotta cookies

My feeling of empowerment is short-lived.

The next morning, Jane storms into our house with Bianca and Robin shuffling behind her like scolded children. I want to vomit because Robin has never looked so nervous. If she cares what Jane has to say, this is serious. I squeeze a hideous snowman mug I made in middle school in art class, hoping I don't squeeze hard enough to break it; it's ugly but still my creation.

"What the hell were you two thinking?" Jane's yells. Her red lacquer nails seem poised to slash angrily at someone, causing me and Mom to step back.

Mom pulls me half-behind her. "Do not yell at my daughter! They should've thought before they did what they did but what's done is done. Besides, nothing they said was wrong." She looks at Bianca, whose red face is covered in tears and snot. My heart squeezes with guilt.

Jane shoves her phone in Mom's face. "Articles like this disagree. They think this is a cry for attention, a sign that Robin is quitting! She mentions her 'true passion' is writing movies." She uses air quotes. "They take that to mean she's throwing her acting career away!"

Robin clenches her fists. "There's no reason I can't do both. So, what else are people whining about?"

Jane whirls on her. "I could go on forever! There are people who don't believe the story about that Santa, who think you're lying about your exes and family, and who think you're lying about your panic attacks to gain sympathy."

"None of that is a lie!" Robin shouts, lips quivering. "Aren't you supposed to be on my side?"

"I'm not saying this stuff. This is what other people believe! I have to work a freaking miracle to do damage control! Do you know that your exes and some coworkers are threatening you? If not lawsuits, then their own stories so they can try to control the narrative."

"I didn't even name anybody!"

"But people can figure it out. Do you ever think before you act?"

Bianca shouts, "That's enough!"

Jane's eyes turn into slits. Bianca yelps but she goes on. "You've already fired me, so glare all you want. Robin isn't the first celebrity to come out with her truth. She'll be fine. Maybe you should leave and cool off." She points to the door.

Jane gapes. Robin whistles, Mom's eyes widen, and I feel my jaw drop. Jane recomposes herself before turning to me. "You will have no further contact with Robin. You're fired. You'll be lucky if nobody comes after you for your role in this stunt. You were supposed to keep an eye on her, not encourage her recklessness. I should've listened to my gut when it said not to trust you."

Mom says, "Is your gut telling you to shut up before I throw you out into the snow? If not, then this is your warning. I couldn't be prouder of these girls. Too bad you can't do the same. It's because of managers like you that the toxic culture of media can continue."

Jane clenches her teeth. "Let's go, Robin. We'll continue this discussion on the way to the inn."

She slams the door behind her, causing a wreath with ugly gnomes to fall. Mom raises a brow as she puts the wreath back then takes it back off. "I'm not a fan of this. What was I thinking? This is a sign to take it down. That mean woman has done at least one thing right."

If her goal is to lighten the mood, she failed. I turn to Bianca. She cuts me off before I can speak by holding her hand up. "Do not talk to me. You got me fired, Ellie. I was finally doing well and I was finally happy until you ruined it. You ruin everything!"

Bianca sobs on her way out. Mom follows her. Robin hands me a tissue as I cry.

"We didn't do anything wrong." But she doesn't sound sure. That makes me cry harder. She glances between me and the door. "I don't have a choice but to go. Hang in there."

I'm left alone. I've made a fool of myself to the world, ruined Bianca's career, and failed at my job to keep Robin out of trouble.

I head outside, unsure what I can do. I just feel like I have to say something to Jane. I have to do something so I don't collapse in despair.

They are standing outside what I presume is Jane's car, the shiniest car I've seen in town. I halt as I hear what they are saying. They don't whisper as nobody is on the street and they're not talking loud enough for anyone to eavesdrop. Well, anyone except me as I hide behind the truck parked in front of Jane's car.

"You at least should think about your parents' debt. If you're blacklisted because nobody trusts you not to badmouth them, how will you pay their debts?" Jane says.

"That shouldn't be my problem."

"We both know you never say no, no matter how much I tell you to cut them off." Jane softens until her ice-cold exterior comes back. "And if you're serious about writing, being blacklisted could impact that."

Robin wipes her eyes. "Just tell me what I need to do."

Jane grabs Robin's shoulders. "You're going to apologize for it, blame it on a mental breakdown, say you're going to a hospital, and say it was Ellie's idea."

Robin shoves her hands off. "What the hell? I'm not going to a hospital! It wasn't a breakdown. I'm not pinning this on Ellie. We both came up with it."

That's not totally the truth. I would appreciate that if my stomach were not in a thousand knots. My heart thunders in my ears. I can't believe Jane wants Robin to throw me under the bus. Well, I can, but still. My blood boils like water for pasta.

"We'll talk more on the way back. Get in." Jane ushers her into the passenger seat.

I collapse in tears on the couch when I get inside. Heartburn and overheating torture me as I think of the worst-case scenarios: getting sued, getting stalked for interviews, trolls telling me I'm overreacting about ableism, Bianca never forgiving me, or Robin hanging me out to dry.

The thing about anxiety is that I can't control my thoughts. I get sucked into them and spiral like I'm water going down a drain. Even when I know things aren't likely and I know I'm catastrophizing, I can't make it stop. Also, it's hard to tell myself nothing bad will happen when I've screwed up so royally.

Mom hugs me. She's quiet because she knows when I need a lecture and when I just need held. After a few minutes, she pulls me up. "Let's make cookies."

Baking ricotta cookies is one of our traditions. The sweet scents of sugar from the mixture and the mixture for the frosting remind me there is still some good in the world. But I'm quiet as Mom chatters about a TV show she wants us to try, funny stories from work (at least *she* finds funny), and so on in a failed effort to distract me. I'm robotic from mixing to putting the cookies in the oven.

It is when I decline a hot chocolate that Mom has had enough. "Oh, god. This is serious if you're rejecting hot chocolate. I know it's hard for you to control your emotions but you need to put things in perspective. Things will be okay. Have I ever been wrong about that?"

"No." And I mean it. Still, I cry again. "Sorry I'm a crybaby. It's just that I'm used to people tossing me aside. I don't know if Bianca will forgive me. Most of all, I hate that I've screwed up yet again. It's what I'm best at."

She forces me to meet her eyes. "That's not true. Your blog is good." She puts her finger on my lips when I begin to protest. "It's just hard for things to stand out online, even great things. You're good at being a friend. Robin sure needed one."

"A friend wouldn't have gotten her in trouble."

"She made her choice. It seems like it was her idea anyway. I don't think she'll do what Jane wants." She smirks at my wide eyes. "You weren't the only one eavesdropping. I would give Robin the benefit of the doubt."

Easy for her to say but it's not worth arguing. I'm so tired I let Mom steer me to the couch, give me Italian hot chocolate, and turn on a made-for-TV holiday movie. I mumble a negative when she asks if I plan to write a review. It's the first time I haven't considered reviewing a film. Things are indeed dire.

The final sign of how serious my misery has become is when the only thing that brings me an iota of serenity is burrowing under at least five fuzzy blankets with fuzzy slippers like I can hide from my problems.

CHAPTER 13

Holiday tradition: cozy sweater

A cozy sweater is perfect for warmth and hiding.

The blue sweater doesn't hide me but I feel safe like a turtle in a shell in oversized clothes. It's one of my methods of feeling secure when I feel like the world is out to get me. It helps when the stress ball and the somewhat-helpful breathing exercises aren't enough. It doesn't stop people from staring and whispering but I feel less exposed in a too-big sweater if that makes any sense. I imagine I can hide in it like a turtle in a shell.

Loose sweaters have been my uniform for the past few days. It's been three days since Jane and Robin left. I've seen nothing in the media, so I dare to hope that Mom is right about Robin having my back.

Unfortunately, Jane was right about former colleagues and exes feeling slighted by Robin. My anxiety was right about trolls messaging me or leaving comments saying I don't appreciate neurotypical allyship just because I called out ableism. For the first time I've had to block people, and it's scary.

I've written and deleted so many messages to Robin, who hasn't contacted me since leaving my house. I'm tired of always being the one to reach out to people first, and I don't know if Jane will do something to instill the fear of God into me if I reach out. The lack of response from Robin hurts.

Nicole yanks my phone out of my hands. "No more reading the comments, doom scrolling, or whatever you're doing." She puts my phone in her backpack. "You don't have to live up to your shirt's words." She points to the frowny face on my sweater.

"It's on point. But fine." I stab my salad. "I'll pretend I'm fine. So, how are you?" I ask dryly.

I've sat with Alice, Nicole, and their friends for the past few days. Alice has revealed her insecurities in comparison to Candace, saying she knows she'll never be manager or owner of the store due to lack of business savvy but is happy doing art. She's made art for her mom and sister to sell at the store. Her eyes sparkle like her jewelry whenever she talks about art.

Nicole and I have gotten closer too. I've visited her at the library to discuss books since nobody was behind me at the circulation desk. Since then, Nicole and I have talked in Biology class as promised and I've added some of her book recs to my TBR while she's promised to look into my movie and show recs. We've followed each other's blogs and socials, and share each other's content. Nicole has shared ideas with the librarians at the public library on what books to put on display after I encouraged her.

Alice, her friends, Nicole, and I have a lot in common from books to TV shows, and they happily listen to my recommendations as well as what to avoid. They asked me questions about Robin at first until I stated I had no interest in talking about her and asked them to respect that, which they have. Hilary never would have done that.

I forgot how wonderful it is to spend time with people I like and vice versa. They are open to activity suggestions based on my blog posts. For example, Alice is open to hiking after I saw it in a movie about a wellness retreat. I forgot how exciting it is to look forward to something *with* somebody.

"So, my store is getting more traffic but barely." Alice stirs the straw in her soda cup. "I should've listened when people told me art is hard to sell."

I accept a piece of her mother's tonkatsu that she lets me try. "Don't give up. I wanted to give up on my blog lots of times. But I also had a celebrity help promote it, so it's different for me." Will I ever stop putting my foot in my mouth?

"I know I'll be okay. I'm just glad my parents finally got on board with my plans to major in art."

"I got my parents to support my English degree, so the sky is the limit," Nicole says. Her russet-colored eyes widen at something on her phone. She hesitantly meets my eyes.

I feel my heart race. I recognize the "Should I tell her?" look. "What is it? Just tell me."

She hands me the phone like she's handing me a piranha. My heart plummets into my stomach as I read the article, in which Robin has released a statement. Jane has released it on her behalf, saying Robin is too nervous to speak to the public. Apparently, Robin has apologized for her "hurtful words" and admits she "overreacts" to things, which is why she'll go to more therapy, maybe even a hospital.

The last line lights a fire under my feet that makes me run out of the cafeteria faster than a jaguar, not caring that I might have hit Alice with my backpack as I snatched it.

Manners are easy to overlook even for chronic people pleasers when it comes to anxiety.

I sit on a toilet in the bathroom, putting my head between my legs. The last part of Robin's statement breaks through the sound of blood rushing in my ears when nothing else can: "Ellie is entitled to her truth and I hope she rethinks her words, too."

Cold anger overruns the heated blood of panic rushing through me enough to enable me to make a call.

"Hello? Ellie?"

"I saw your statement. You were full of crap when you told me to stand up to the world, weren't you?" I don't pause between words so I fear she doesn't understand.

But she does. "Ellie, I was under so much pressure. I didn't exactly deny anything."

My voice cracks as my eyes water. "Yes, you did! Don't gaslight me! You think I'll just buy whatever you say because I'm autistic? You wouldn't be the first!"

"What? God no! I don't think that."

"You did deny what you said." My voice cracks as hot tears run down my cheeks. "You didn't say 'I didn't say these things' but you made excuses. You didn't even have the guts to say it yourself. You had Jane do it." The only reason my shaking had doesn't drop the phone is because it's gripping it so hard.

"You don't get it! I could've been blackballed. That would've impacted my movie writing, too, because nobody would've wanted to work with someone who publicly badmouths colleagues. I don't like my parents but they're still my parents, and they still have debts I need to help with. My exes threatened to sue me."

"I know all that! Why do you cling to it when you're so damn miserable? You're smart. You can figure out a way to write movies and speak the truth."

"Oh, like you're so courageous?" she snaps. "You're likeable but you're afraid to make friends or get another job because of bad experiences. I get back on the horse after every terrible experience I've had, so why can't you?"

"You need to stop talking. Like, right now. You can't understand my life like I can't understand yours. At least I've stopped trying to please people."

"Instead, you just avoid them. Very good alternative," she scoffs.

"Screw you, Robin! At least I'm not a traitor! Agreeing to keep an eye on you is the worst mistake I ever made!"

There is a pause on her end. "Oh, yeah? Well, I wish a troll had babysat me instead of you! The troll wouldn't whine as much!"

"Glass house!"

I hang up with a growl. I kick the stall door, swearing as my foot pays the price. Standing up for myself should feel awesome but I'm nauseous instead.

*

A floor can be made comfortable with the right tools.

I plop myself on the floor and press my back into the end of my bed when things are really bad. A sweater that is warm from just coming out of the dryer is draped around my shoulders as I hug my legs. One of my comfort shows, *Parks and Recreation*, plays on the TV on top of my dresser. Keeping me company are stuffed animals on another dresser and bobbleheads of my favorite movie characters from Elphaba to Princess Fiona. And, of course, hot chocolate, which I already drained from a snowman mug. I don't meet the eyes of any of the inanimate objects for fear they secretly have souls that are judging me for being so weak.

The door opens but the voice doesn't belong to Mom. "Ellie?" Bianca says. She sits next to me and touches the sweater. "Oh, so warm. I love warm laundry."

"So do I. Why are you here?"

"I'm sorry for what I said. I was upset, justifiably. But I've done some thinking and maybe this career isn't for me. Even if I become great at it, do I want to be like Jane? I know what it's like to be made to feel small and I don't want to do that to people like Robin. I could put my public relations degree to other uses. I'm figuring it out. Mom supports me but no surprise there."

"That's good" is all I can mumble, afraid there will be a "but" somewhere.

Bianca wraps an arm around my shoulders. "I shouldn't have yelled at you. Can you forgive me?"

"*Me* forgive *you*? I'm sorry for messing things up. Not even drinking hot chocolate filled with caramel, sprinkles, and whipped cream could cheer me up." I point to the empty mug.

"Oh, wow. Something hot chocolate couldn't help? This is serious." Bianca laughs but frowns when I don't laugh too. "I'll be fine. Like I said, this was a wake-up call. You did me a favor."

"I doubt that. All I do is make people's lives inconvenient at best and terrible at worst."

"That is not true. It is time to stop putting other people's comfort before your own. As you and I know, making people comfortable at the expense of our own isn't worth it. And I think some of our insecurity and desire to prove to people that we're needed stems from our crummy dad leaving us." She wipes a tear from her eye. "In some ways, you're lucky you don't have as many memories of him as I do. But it's his loss because we are awesome people who don't need to prove anything to him or anyone. The person's approval that matters most is your own."

I lean my head against her should, sniffling. "I guess I'll always have the instinct to prove my worth but I'm trying to unlearn.

Public scrutiny has ruined my digestive system but the thought of taking back what I said is even more unbearable. "I'm not taking back a thing. Actually, I have an idea."

Bianca grins as I tell her the idea. Mom checks on us so we fill her in. I have her eager support. Mixed with the anticipation is pride.

CHAPTER 14

Holiday tradition: decorate a gingerbread house

Making videos is not our specialty.

Bianca, Mom and I thought it'd be easy to create a good quality video like any influencer. Apparently, we didn't take into account lighting, what my good angles are, and unwanted items in the background like my pile of laundry that needs to get put away. We settle for me standing against my wall with the least terrible lighting and nothing but the wall and single-word decals like "Dream" and "Act." I wipe milk from my cereal from my mouth before I tell Bianca to begin recording.

I clench a stuffed axolotl in my hands to center myself since all anybody can see are my shoulders and head. Certain times call for squeezing stuffed animals instead of stress balls.

"Hi, everyone." God, I should've taken Bianca's advice to rehearse instead of insisting on unfiltered authenticity. I try to make my voice less squeaky and avoid putting question marks at the end of every sentence. Here's hoping all those terrible class presentations will pay off. "I'm Ellie Conti. I'll get to the point. I was asked by Robin Darcy's manager to keep an eye on her while she tried to fix her image. At first, I was terrified because I'm not good at exiting my comfort zone. Then we got close. I was coming out of my shell, and then we got criticized for the little speech we gave a few days ago."

Bianca nods at me to keep going. Mom steps forward but stops herself, knowing she can't baby me. I'm so scared I'll cause more trouble but there's no going back. This is live.

"I've gotten comments and messages from people saying ableist things and demanding I put them in touch with Robin. People focus on that more than my movie reviews. I'm here to say…" I swallow the boulder-sized lump in my throat. "I'm here to say enough is enough. Neither of us owes you anything."

The heat that courses through me thinking of the times Robin was sad and felt so alone gives me the strength to go on. "Instead of assuming someone hates the holidays, think about what they're going through. It's okay not to be jolly during the holidays. In fact, you need to think about the harms of toxic positivity and reevaluate your perception of celebrity culture."

I blink back tears as I think about how I just stood up for Robin while she doesn't have my back. "I don't regret anything I said in the video you no doubt saw. I'm tired of making people comfortable. I'm tired of escaping into TV instead of living life because I'm afraid of messing up or getting hurt. I try new activities based on movies but I need to try things that are truly risky like trusting people outside my mom and sister. That's not to say I'll stop reviews!" I say quickly, not wanting to ruin any chance my blog has left of thriving. "And, by the way, consider supporting small accounts like mine instead of focusing only on big accounts like celebrity accounts. Also support small businesses or accounts, especially by marginalized creators. There are two I can give right now that belong to two friends of mine." I give them the information on Alice's store and Nicole's socials. "The holidays are about being better people, right? It's not fair to ask someone like Robin to be better if you don't put in the work yourself. That's all. Thank you."

Bianca stops recording. I slide down the wall to the floor and hug the axolotl so hard I'm glad it's not a living creature. Mom and Bianca sit on either side of me, telling me how proud they are.

After about half an hour of helping me calm down from the overwhelming sensations, Mom and Bianca leave to prepare for decorating a gingerbread house.

"Why do we make it every year? We don't like gingerbread." I wrinkle my nose.

"The candy we put on it is good. Also, it's fun," Bianca says. "Meet us in the kitchen."

It takes herculean effort to ignore the notifications on my phone when I take it out of my pocket. I text Alice to tell Doris I'm interested in interviewing for the job. I ask her if she wants to hang out outside of school sometime. I'm risking rejection again from a job and a potential friend but I feel unstoppable after what I just did. Maybe I'll even come to like gingerbread.

I'm proven wrong after I try eating a piece of the gingerbread house when we finish decorating it. The house is a train wreck with most of the candy falling off, the icing cracking apart, and the front of the house looking like a face screaming in pain. But that doesn't matter as long as I have Mom and Bianca.

CHAPTER 15

Holiday tradition: heart-to-hearts

My first Saturday shift wasn't too bad.

I began work Thursday after school, and I took forever to do change at the cash register because of my terrible math skills, I spilled a coffee order, and I mixed up the orders of two people named Sarah (in my defense it's one of the most common names). Otherwise, work is good. Doris, Emilio, Alice, and two other workers are patient with me. They don't get annoyed when I ask for clarification or act like I'm questioning authority when I ask why we do things a certain way. I'm not screamed at for accidentally offending a customer, which I did when I was anxious by juggling filling coffee, fielding a customer complaint, and a guy telling me to move faster.

The Saturday shift has the most customers, so this break is much-needed. I'm already on my third cup of tea today; I'm cutting back on hot chocolate and trying to drink healthier as Alice has encouraged by sharing her green tea bags. But I treat myself to a well-deserved scone.

Alice taps her "Couldn't care less" mug against my "Company is overrated" mug. "You survived your first Saturday morning shift! How do you feel?"

"Crummy but proud. I still fear I'll mess up but I'm not scared I'll get fired. It's a nice feeling, even if my feet don't feel great."

Alice looks at something on her phone and her eyebrows furrow. She hesitantly looks at me. "Robin just made a video statement and people are going wild over it. I can unfollow if you want."

"You don't have to do that. Can we watch it? I'll probably regret it but I need to see it." And hear what she has to say. She can't hurt me more than she already has, or that's what I tell my nausea.

Robin obviously thinks it's a bad idea but honors my request by hitting play on her phone. My heart squeezes when I lay eyes upon Robin for the first time in days even via screen. For once, she's not wearing makeup and black circles are underneath her eyes. She stands in front of the heater in her inn room.

She clears her throat. "So, hi. I need to say this before I lose my nerve." She closes her eyes as if bracing herself. "I didn't mean a word of my recent apology. I won't apologize for calling people out, and I don't get why people want to sue me considering I named nobody or gave enough details to identify anyone. I don't want any of you playing detective to figure out who. I want you to spend time thinking about what I said about how poisonous this industry and public opinion can be. I am mindful of the privileges I have as a white, cisgender woman, so I know I face less struggle than those who do not have my privileges."

She takes a deep breath. "I'm quitting acting. I'll finish up this last movie and I'm not renewing contracts. I'm going to focus on writing shows and movies with stories people don't often see even in this day and age. I could write plotlines with bisexual actresses struggling with mental health, the kinds of stories I could have used when I was young. I can write stories where the main love of the plot isn't even romantic. True love can be friendship. Tossing away that type of friendship is one of my biggest regrets. This friend and my time here helped me rethink my life."

Her eyes glisten as I'm sure mine do. Alice squeezes my hand as Robin continues. "Ellie, if you're watching this, I'm sorry for everything. You did nothing wrong. I wish I were as strong as you."

Me? Strong? She must be joking. Hot tears plop into my teacup as this unbelievable thing happens. I'm torn between holding on to my anger and wanting to hug her through the phone.

Emilio and Doris have wandered over. Doris squeezes my shoulder while Emilio just stands next to me.

"I won't apologize for having a complicated relationship with the holidays. I won't be shamed for panic attacks, for being bisexual, or for speaking the truth. The holidays are about miracles. Gaining the courage to speak up is one of the biggest miracles of all. That's it. Thanks for listening."

The overwhelming torrent of emotions threatens to make me explode. My hands squeeze my mug until Emilio removes it.

"When I'm overwhelmed, I take a walk outside," he says.

"I do that a lot. I can do that now." I check my phone. "Five minutes until break is over." I'm as monotone as a robot.

"Yes, take a walk. And don't worry if you're a minute late," Doris says. "Do what you need to do."

"No, no. I can calm down enough to get back to work like any other person."

"Ellie, everyone has days where they need to cool off. Now go." She pushes me out the door.

I and Emilio offer to come with me. I need to be alone when cooling off. I literally cool off in the frigid air, which makes me go back in for my coat. I walk quickly and focus on my surroundings. I'm grounded back to reality by counting how many parking spots are available on the street (zero), noticing a wreath in danger of falling off a streetlamp, and noticing for the first time how the snow has thinned into a layer of gray slush on the grass and sidewalks.

Now I'm calm enough to process Robin's video. I want to hold on to anger because anger makes me feel less vulnerable and less likely to allow someone to hurt me again. I think of people who have broken their promises and tossed me aside like she did. However, a different montage of memories reminds me that Robin is the first person to acknowledge she hurt me and to say I did nothing wrong.

I read the comments under the video as I walk back to the café. Some people accuse her of seeking attention;

others are rooting for her. A few commenters dedicate paragraphs to sharing their struggles with panic attacks, lack of happy holiday memories, and so on.

One commenter points out how much she risked by doing this. I look around, wondering if Robin thinks her efforts to improve her public image were thrown away after renouncing her apology. But it may not have been a waste if she meant what she said about finding a true friend in me and that I, as well as the town, helped her reevaluate her life choices.

The thoughts clogging my head like cotton cause me to spill coffee (thankfully iced), bump into the counter, and look at the door every so often like Robin will stroll in. People who recognize me ask what I think about Robin's video, whether I'll forgive her, if I'll make my own video, and so on until I snap.

"I'm not answering any Robin questions!"

The café becomes so silent we can only hear a kid chewing on his cookie, obvious to or not caring about the tense atmosphere. I fear this is something even Doris cannot excuse but she motions for me to continue. "You should only ask questions about coffee and treats. If you're not buying anything, then we have to ask you to leave. Yeah, I'm looking at you, the guy who cut the line without even ordering something."

A few people groan as they leave empty-handed. The remaining customers have the good sense to listen to her, turning back to their phones or conversations.

Doris high-fives me. "That was awesome!"

"I'm sorry if I hurt the business."

"No, no! I have to yell at a roomful of customers at least once a week. They still come back. My treats are too good to pass up. You should leave early."

"No way! I'm fine."

"You're not, and I think you have something more important to do. Talk to Robin."

I twist my apron. "I don't know."

"Considering what she just did, you can at least go see her. Go!"

She shoos me into the break room to get my stuff. I look to my coworkers for help reasoning with her but Emilio shakes his head, Alice mouths "No way," and the other two employees busy themselves with tasks. I narrow my eyes at all of them.

I walk home as I decide whether to stay home or do what Doris says. Nobody wants me to hide at home, as Mom and Bianca make clear as they materialize in the doorway and tell me to see Robin.

"I'll go with you if you want," Bianca offers. "Since I'm unemployed, I have more time now." She still can't say it without a wince despite trying to be nonchalant.

"Or you can figure out what you want to do next while I catch up on this holiday miniseries I started."

"Nope. You're marching your ass to that inn. Even if you don't make up, get some closure," Mom orders, pointing an ugly spinach-colored nail at my car. She catches me staring.

"I wanted to try a new color. I'll replace the color while you're gone."

I growl. "I'm surprised. Usually you want to get back at the people who hurt me."

"I'm not condoning what she did. However, I get she was between a rock and a hard place. I also know she's the first genuine friend you've ever had. You're probably hers, too. Now go!"

They wave at me as I open my car door. I roll my eyes at both of them. But it only takes a few minutes in my car and on the mostly empty roads for fantasies of payback to be replaced by wishes that are painful to make. Am I hoping for too much to reconcile with Robin? Did she mean what she said or was she just trying to look good by saying how much she valued her friendship with me? She came to Madison Grove to say what people want to hear. I'd be naïve to assume I'm exempt.

I try to toss these thoughts away like snowballs. Robin revealed things to me she didn't tell anyone else. I know her well enough that she doesn't like being vulnerable, and making that video must have been difficult.

If I were Robin, I can't say what I would have done if Jane told me what to do. Robin was right about me not understanding, which gives me a twinge of guilt. I need to apologize too.

Someone raps on my window as soon as I park, causing me to jump. I don't necessarily relax upon seeing Jane's frantic face.

"Look, you can't talk me out of seeing Robin." It feels so good not to care what an authority figure thinks.

Her forehead is covered in lines. "You can't talk to her if you can't find her! Robin's gone missing. I've been calling, texting, and even messaging her but no response. She's not in her room and she left her phone! God, this is the beginning of a true crime documentary!"

A pit the size of New Jersey forms in my stomach. "She's missing? For how long?"

"I tried getting in touch this morning but no response. God, I wouldn't have to do so much if I still had Bianca."

"Then maybe you shouldn't have fired her."

Her jaw tightens. "I'm not getting into it. You and she both made bad choices."

"And you didn't? Honestly, why do you care where Robin is or isn't? I figured you'd drop her after she made that video, going back on what you told her to do."

She sighs. "I know you think I'm a dragon lady, and I am but I do care about my clients. I also cared about Bianca. I do things because I know how the world works."

"But you're part of the problem." I need to focus. "Any ideas where Robin could be?"

"None! She doesn't have a car because everyone has been driving her."

I look at the trail I took Robin to not long ago. This seems like a cliché from a heartwarming movie but what do we have to lose? "I'm going to check out a place I've shown her. Couldn't hurt."

"I'll come with you." She holds up her hand when I start to protest. "No use arguing with me. Let's go."

She struts ahead of me, then slows down so I can take the lead. Her six-inch heels don't help either with the ice and gravel. Her eyes narrow at my smirk.

The trail is empty save for squirrels and litter. I'd be heartbroken about the lack of care for the environment if I weren't a tornado of worry for Robin. What the hell is she thinking? I hate giving Jane credit for anything but she's right that taking off without her phone is practically begging for a true crime documentary. I twist a thick stick in my hands to deal with the horrendous idea of a podcast host discussing the chain of events that led up to this.

Enough, anxiety. I will not spiral, at least not until I find Robin. The stick breaks in my hands, breaking the quiet and making birds flee.

I hear snow crunch nearby. I look to the right of the path to see a figure atop the rock who has turned to look at us. Robin stares at us with red eyes and an equally red nose.

"Thank god! You had everyone worried to death!" Jane says. "Let's get you back to the inn."

"I'm done listening to you. Go away." She turns back around with a sniffle.

"Come on, Robin. You can't pull stunts like this."

"Can you lay off a little?" I snap. I whisper, "Let me talk to her."

Her lips press into a thin line but she caves in after a glance at Robin, who is so hunched she might fall forward. She gestures for me to approach Robin.

There is enough room on the boulder for me to sit next to Robin. I endure the cold, rugged surface for Robin's sake. I notice the paper cup of hot chocolate in her hand.

She sees me looking. "You said hot chocolate makes anything better. It didn't help, since hot chocolate reminds me of you, and that reminds me of what I did to you."

"But you tried to make it right. That video you made was badass. I hope you don't get into too much trouble." I hope she doesn't notice how much I fidget from the coldness of my butt.

"On top of my parents disowning me, the fact nobody will take me seriously as a writer, and I may have no money for college after getting sued, how can things get worse?"

What should I say? None of my social skills lessons prepared me for this situation. I guess I'll have to wing it.

"I don't know what will happen but I'll be there for you. It sucks your parents still suck but maybe it's good not to be involved with them anymore. If enough time passes, I'm sure people will look at your scripts. You're talented, and you'll be irresistible if you hone your craft. Jane is…Jane but she might help you figure stuff out regarding the backlash."

I angle my body toward her. "I hate not having a plan. I need routine and the predictable to feel safe in a world that often makes me feel unsafe. But the past few weeks have taught me that the unpredictable can be beautiful, even with risks. I've been hit with the cons of risk-taking, and although it hurt, I'm now less scared of taking chances. I'm less scared of taking chances because now I know I'm strong enough to endure."

Where was this poetic language during my creative writing assignments? At least it seems to be reaching Robin, who finally looks at me. She wipes her face with the sleeves of her coat.

"You're strong, too. But it's okay to be vulnerable, too, which is why so many people appreciate what you said. You came to this town to improve your image and to appear less flawed. But you ended up showing people that we should stop pretending to be flawless or happy when we're not. I think you can sway the court of public opinion if you haven't already."

A sob that echoes through the wintry landscape startles me so I almost fall off the boulder. Did I make things worse? My chest clenches until Robin throws aside her cup of hot chocolate to hug me.

"I'm so glad to have you in my life." A sniffle. "You promise you'll be there no matter how bad things may get?

I'm sorry for being needy. I'm sorry I wasted hot chocolate. That must be a sin to you."

"Not if it was bad. You're not being needy. I meant every word I said. I changed my life, too, though not as radically as yours. Can we please stand up before my butt gets frozen to this boulder?"

I tell Robin the changes I've made to my life as we rejoin Jane. Robin says, "We're both pretty badass." She turns to Jane with crossed arms. "Nothing you say will change my mind about anything."

"I know. I'm just glad you're okay." She chuckles at our astonishment. "I'm not a warm and fuzzy person but I'm not a monster. I want to apologize to both of you. While you two were talking, I called Bianca to apologize."

My eyes widen. "You really did that?"

"Yup. I was stunned when she declined to work for me again. It's her choice." She shrugs before turning to Robin. "I won't beg you to keep acting. It's your life. If you want, I can get you in touch with writers, see if they'd want to give you advice. I recommend you take some classes. Talent alone isn't enough."

Robin grins. "Wow. Thanks. I'm not used to this version of you."

"Don't get used to it. Now, let's go and figure out the next steps. I've been bombarded with interview requests."

Jane goes on about ideas we care nothing about. Robin rubs her forehead. "I really created a mess. Time to face the consequences. I apologize in advance if people bother you because of me."

I square my shoulders. "Then they can bring it on. I found one thing that makes me jolly: standing up for myself."

She laughs. "I've found some holiday cheer after all since coming to town. It's called doing things my way."

CHAPTER 16

Holiday tradition: New Year's Ball Drop

The weather is never predictable in New Jersey.

Random ice patches and puddles are all that remain of the snow despite it being New Year's Eve. Sure, the roads are safer and it's warm enough to ditch winter coats but I miss the beauty of the winter wonderland. At least I'm not freezing my butt off on the town hall's lawn where everyone crowds for the fireworks and free snacks.

It's cool enough to warrant sweaters but warm enough to ditch winter coats. Thus, I wear my penguin onesie; I like to end the new year in cute, comfortable style as a sign to the universe to make the coming year cozy if not fantastic. Robin laughed at my outfit but glared at a guy who picked on me, especially for "waddling like a penguin." It helps she's wearing a reindeer onesie not only in solidarity with me, Bianca and Mom but as part of her self-care, "I-don't-care-what-people-think" routine.

I wrinkle my nose after sipping the hot chocolate from a paper cup. "I get saving money by bulk-buying packets, but they could've at least offered whipped cream or milk at that hot chocolate station."

"You're such a hot chocolate snob. It is still doing its job of bringing people together," Robin says, though she hasn't taken more than a sip of hers.

Robin is the most relaxed I've seen her since our talk on the path. She only did one interview with Patricia Jones to discuss what's next. Patricia was supportive and addressed the audience to encourage people to end mental health stigma.

Since then, Robin has looked at classes or schools for film-writing and has talked with people that Jane connected her with. Nobody has gone through with suing her, although she did get texts "warning" her not to name names. She ignored them. She's made posts online about panic attacks and encouraging people to seek help.

"I really needed this. All this stuff helps with the disguise so nobody bothers me," she says, pointing to the party hat on top of her gold wig and the beaded necklaces dangling from her neck.

"I needed an escape from reality, too," Bianca says.

Candace takes Bianca's hand. "Your reality isn't that bad, is it?" she teases.

"Not with you in it."

I gag as they peck each other on the lips but it's adorable. They've been spending a lot of time together and Bianca has ideas on how to put that public relations degree to use, like journalism, preferably covering the happy stuff versus doomscrolling material.

Alice and Emilio were with us until they took off together, which they've been doing a lot lately. It's not hard to figure out they like each other, especially after I caught them kissing in an alley at work. I don't mind since Alice still lets me sit with her at lunch and we've hung out once outside of work and school. Emilio and I made plans to meet up outside of work, too, and he has talked nonstop about his plans to perform cover songs online and either become a musician or music teacher someday.

Nicole waves at me from where she stands with her parents, cousins, and relatives. We chatted, took selfies, then she showed her relatives. They don't get to see each other often since they live in Miami, so I understand why she's focused on them. Nicole gave me a book she won in a giveaway and wouldn't take no for an answer, as she feels grateful for the increase in Followers since my shoutout in my video. Before she left, she confided that she's working on her own book.

My phone is blissfully still and silent. I was plagued with nonstop calls, texts, emails, and DMs for interviews and anything related to Robin. But some have said how much they like my blog and two other blogs have requested guest posts. Jane sent me an email with a list of schools with the best film studies or journalism programs. I'm still weary of her considering the crap she put us through but she's trying. Some are the same schools Robin is looking at, so I'm excited at the possibility of going to school together.

"My reality isn't that bad either," I say. I am both competent and happy at my job. School is going great with people noticing me more but not bothering me except to compliment my blog or suggest something to review.

Nothing is perfect. All of us still have problems to figure out and ways to improve ourselves. But what matters is that we try, and we don't underestimate ourselves. Also, perfect is overrated, emphasized by the ketchup from the hot dog that gets on my white scarf.

"Seriously, honey?" Mom groans. "I just bought that for you!"

"No use crying over things we can't change. That's what you taught me," I remind her with an impish grin.

She softly pats me with a fake angry face but then kisses me on the head. "Messiness aside, I'm so proud of you."

"Enough of the sappiness! The countdown is starting!" Robin tells us. The she adds, "I'm proud of both of us."

The countdown has started from ten. So many thoughts go through my head with the last of this year. For once, I don't dwell on what I messed up and wish for a time machine. I thank my mistakes for making me stronger and appreciate what went right. I look toward the upcoming year with excitement.

Fireworks light up the winter sky to cheers. Everyone hugs. Robin hugs me the longest.

"You ready for what this year will bring?" she asks.

I'm a hundred percent confident when I respond, "You bet I am."

Acknowledgements

A book cannot be created and released to the world alone. That's why I'm giving a shout-out to everyone who helped make *Hot Chocolate and Holiday Mishaps* possible.

A shout-out to the friends who read and critiqued my manuscript.

Thank you to Starr Baumann at Quiethouse Editing for editing, and thank you to Leigh from Quiethouse Editing for beta reading.

The wonderful cover you see was designed by Hannah Linder of Hannah Linder Designs.

Thank you to everyone on social media who shared posts related to the book; for example, sharing the cover reveal post.

Shoutout to everyone who allowed me the honor of an author interview.

Thank you to my ARC readers.

And last but definitely not least, I thank my family, especially my mom.

Finally, thank you to my readers for giving my book a chance.

About the Author

Samantha Picaro is an author of Young Adult novels including *Limitless Roads Café, Recipe for Confidence* and *Hot Chocolate and Holiday Mishaps.* She is also an avid reader who is passionate about highlighting books that are self-published and books that are not as well-known as popular books.

When not writing, you can find her trying new coffee flavors, reading (of course), and volunteering for various causes. She lives in New Jersey.

Learn more about Samantha and join her newsletter list for news, book recommendations, and more!

Website: www.samanthapicarowrites.com

Instagram: @author.samantha.picaro

Facebook: Author Samantha Picaro

Goodreads: Samantha Picaro

TikTok: @authorsamanthapicaro